# STALKING MY LOVE...

**RUCHI CHANDRA VERMA**

This book is dedicated to all my wonderful readers, who wait for my books, asking me, prodding me and giving me feedback to do better every single time.

Thank you so much for choosing to spend your time with my book. Your love, appreciation, and support mean the world to me.

Do drop in a note of feedback, rating, and review when you finish this story. It would really make my day brighter!

I am because of you all... Thank you very much!

# Contents

# Foreword

This is a crisp narrative and finely executed story by Ruchi where you will experience going through various emotions. An emotionally charged, enchanting tale of love, courage, responsibilities and togetherness. Definitely an outstanding start for the new series! A must read book that will leave you thoroughly satisfied but impatient for the next book in the series.

- Aashi Irf, Author of Simmering Love

# Acknowledgements

My story cannot be called complete without acknowledging the support from my family and my friends. Throughout the process of thinking, plotting, writing, and re-writing the story, some people stood by me steadfastly lending support, giving ideas, nudging me along, and encouraging me when the flow of words stops.

My family, my husband, and my boy, who put up with my extended hours in front of the laptop when I forget to do chores, or I am too lost in my story world. My son is my most hardcore ardent fan, and I have to write well just for him!

A big shout-out to my author friends and my girls' gang who are always encouraging, helping, and guiding me to write better and bring good stories to you all!

Thank you to each one of you, you all make a lot of difference!
Love you girls!!

# Viraj's Obsession

*Tum meri ho, meri hi rahogi,*

*Tum ban jaao kisi ki bhi Dulhan,*

*Basa lo kisi sang bhi ghar,*

*Par mera pyaar ho, mera junoon,*

*Tum meri ho meri hi rahogi!*

# Prologue

Viraj parked his car under a tree in the shade and sat in it continuing his call. He lifted his left wrist and noted there was still time before he had to drop his precious work and get on with his brotherly duties. He hated stepping out of the comfort of his office in this sweltering Mumbai heat but his brother had left no choice for him today.

Yuvraj had called him, stating that he had met with a minor accident in the college and asked him to come pick him up, as he couldn't ride his bike back home. What Viraj didn't understand was why could he not get home in a cab or as a pillion rider behind one of his useless friends. Anyway, he always roamed around the city with his friends. But being the doting brother that he was, he found himself thoroughly annoyed yet here outside his college finishing his work early to take his brother back home.

Yuvraj was in second year of his college and they were having only practice sessions today for the college festivities which were to begin the next day. Viraj was seven years older than Yuvraj and worked as the Rajvansh Group of Companies CEO. They had ventured into steel, transport, textiles, sugar mills, and construction business lately, all under the capable leadership of Viraj, his father Vikram, and his uncle Vikash.

Viraj sighed as his call came to an end and he stepped out in the scorching hot sun. Damn, his three-piece suit made him sweat even more. He walked across the parking lot to enter the college building. He was not a student but the way he carried himself confidently, the guards instead of questioning his reasons for entry, saluted him and stood erect. This caused several other students to look up and gawk at his handsome stature.

Standing tall at 6 feet 1-inch height, he was lean, muscular and strong. His body had not an inch of fat and he maintained a tough exercise regime to ensure he was always agile and focused. Known as one of the most eligible bachelors in India, he was already a billionaire and a business magnate at the tender age of 27.

He dialled his brother's number only for it to ring without being answered. He cursed under his breath. Time was the most precious commodity he had and he didn't like anyone wasting his time, be it any of his employees or his own brother.

He dialled the number again and barked as soon as the phone was picked up.

"I am here, where are you?"

"Bhai, I am in the basement."

"Basement?" Viraj frowned, why the heck would his brother be in the college basement?

"Yeah, practice sessions are happening in the basement, please come, I am waiting for you!"

Viraj always melted when his brother spoke to him in a gentle pleading voice and Yuvraj knew well how to manipulate his older brother.

As Viraj climbed the stairs down to enter the basement, he realized there were several rooms here, and it wouldn't be easy to search for his brother in all the rooms. He slowly pushed open the door to first room and stood frozen at the sight in front of him.

A tall, slim girl wearing a floral printed pink coloured Anarkali suit was dancing to the beats of a classical song. He stood mesmerized and watched her sway in awe. Her movements were so fluid, so delicate that he wondered if the girl had any bones in her body or if she was made of water. She swirled around once, and then again, she jumped up, landed back on her feet, her hands and feet moving in sync and swirled around continuously at a high speed, her face showing all the emotions that the song portrayed and as she came to a standstill, everyone clapped.

He was not a classical music or dance fan and had never seen any performances prior to this unexpected one. He felt mesmerized, drawn to this beauty who was not just gracious but lithe and danced beautifully. He stood spell bounded and was about to walk up to her, when he realized he was a mere intruder and the dancer didn't know of his presence. He also realized that he was gawking at a college student and felt like a stalker, an old man compared to her. She must be in Yuvraj's batch, a seven- eight year his junior. He took a step back ashamed of himself but he couldn't move away.

She was weaving her magic, making his limbs go weak, his heart go on a rampage in his chest as he focused and memorized each and every detail about her face, her tall slender body and her dress.

A short girl walked up to her and asked something and she turned around, her face towards the door where he stood. He took in a deep breath as her beauty hit something deep within him. So beautiful, so elegant! He was completely bowled over by this diva who was the most beautiful woman he had ever laid his eyes on, and he was no novice when it came to women. She was also the most wonderful dancer he had ever seen in his real life, his mind added.

He stood watching her porcelain face, and her twinkling grey eyes as she laughed at something the girl said and a blush arose on her cheeks. Something flipped in his chest and he was taken over by the urge to be the only one stealing her smiles, making her blush like this.

How would it feel to hold her in my arms, to feel those delicious curves and make her dance just for myself, he mused. He felt a strong sense of possessiveness take over for this stranger, a young girl, he had never seen before.

The dancer turned around, clapped, and motioned for other girls to come stand in a formation and she went around checking their positions and giving them instructions. She helped everyone get in their stance for the practice to begin and played the music.

As the music filled the room yet again, the group of girls began to sway and his eyes stayed riveted on the girl who stood watching everyone else, correcting them but not dancing herself. He willed her to dance yet again, to let him watch her one more time. She shook her head, stopped the music, and corrected a girl's hand movements by showing her the steps all over again. She was the dance teacher, he realized, and immediately felt relief washing over him.

He was not stalking a student; she was at least a teacher here. This made him feel better and he lost himself yet again in watching her serene face, those expressive almond-shaped grey eyes, which he knew if met his gaze would beckon him to drown in them. Her face held a small smile, even when she stopped and corrected a girl, she didn't raise her voice or snap at their mistakes, she gently kept correcting them over and over again.

She turned on the music and turned around and her gaze met his. His heart flipped in his chest and he felt the earth tilt on its axis. She stood rooted in her spot for a few seconds, her forehead crinkling in a frown and then she stepped towards him.

"Who are you?"

He crashed back to reality and took a step back further into the dark corridor.

"I am looking for someone!" He spoke and immediately started walking back towards the next room. The next room had another group of girls practicing drama and he moved to the third room, feeling her unwavering gaze on his back. He wanted to turn back and ask her name but he also knew that he had been caught red-handed watching her and it wouldn't go down well in the college, where he was neither the student nor a teacher not even the owner.

"Bhai, there you are!" Yuvraj's voice reached him and he turned the corner to go see his brother limping toward him with the help of Kishore. He immediately rushed forward and held Yuvraj close as he surveyed the wounds on his brother's legs.

When he walked back towards the exit with his brother, he heard the music playing and the door shut completely. He chuckled as he realized she must have closed the door completely this time to avoid more onlookers.

He didn't like the idea of everyone watching her dance, he didn't like the idea of her being ogled at on the stage by these leering teenagers. She was his and only he could watch her dance and sway.

The next day he found himself galivanting towards the college fest, determined to find more about her. He was glad that with the injured leg, Yuvraj had decided to stay back home and not come to the fest, but he came dressed in casual jeans, a t-shirt, and a denim jacket to try and blend in with the college crowd. He didn't want anyone noticing him or asking what he was doing here. It would create a scandal and scandals he avoided at all costs.

He found a seat in the third row and sat down to watch the stage performances. The fest also had a lot of fun and game activities and stalls at the back but he was not interested in any of it. He was here to watch the girl dance. He had not been able to sleep the previous night, because the moment he closed his eyes he saw her dancing and when he opened his eyes, he saw her walking towards him.

When the classical dance he had seen being practiced the previous day began, his heart broke into a million pieces at the realization that she was not dancing at all. She was just the teacher and she was not here on the stage. Then his heart soared in joy, that all these college kids didn't get to see the most mesmerizing performance of all, and he was the only lucky one to have watched it. He never knew he could feel so many conflicting emotions all at once, he was crushed that he didn't get to see her one more time and he was elated that she was not on the stage being everyone's center of attention either.

He was going to cherish that memory forever and her? He was going to cherish her as well forever!

His beautiful enchantress!

His beautiful muse, who had no name!

His very own *Anamika*.

# CHAPTER ONE

# THE HUSTLE

*Trisha Agarwal*

I scrambled to find my balance as another bike hit my *Activa* from behind, just as I was trying to slow down and take the only parking spot available.

"Hey!" I turned and yelled. I lifted the flap of my helmet to show my face to the bikers.

"Trisha Ma'am! So sorry!" Came the smooth reply and the very next second the helmet was removed to reveal the ever-charming heartthrob of the entire college Yuvraj Rajvansh smiling at me.

I parked my *Activa* and marched straight over to him.

"You come with me!"

"Sorry, I applied brake but the bike took a while to stop. I didn't mean to hit your precious *Dhanno*!"

I controlled the urge to yell back at him to not call my bike as *Dhanno*, that was the name my little sister, Anaisha had given to my *Activa*. And I controlled my urge to yell more at him for hitting me while I was trying to park. There was no use, he wouldn't be bothered and he would just keep smiling at me and working his boyish charm on me, which was absolutely wasted. He didn't faze me at all, he must be three or four years younger than me.

He was, unfortunately, my sister's best friend and her classmate. I was his senior, well now a pass-out graduate of this college, though I was working on a Librarian job here, while I prepared for my fashion designing course exams.

I came from a middle-class background, a few years ago I could have called myself from upper-middle-class family but one tragedy snatched everything away from me. My mother passed away in an accident and my father lost his job at the same time. We had no means of income and I had to grow up overnight to become the bread earner of the family.

A family of a drunkard dad and his three daughters, well actually only two daughters because one daughter, my elder sister was married and lived with her husband now. She was the lucky one among us, she was married and settled by the time our mom passed away and she didn't have to put up with our dad's drunken beatings and thrashings that came mostly my way because I did my best to shield Anaisha, my little angel sister as much as I possibly could.

But Anaisha, or Ana as we all called her was actually no angel, she was the devil incarnate herself. Always up to some mischief and she had found her match in Yuvraj, another devil prankster. I smiled as I thought of their bond, their friendship and often wondered if it was something more and they were both hiding it behind the façade of friendship.

I thought I would be happier if that turned out to be the case. Yuvraj though a prankster, was a gentleman, a rich spoilt prince but with a heart of gold. He belonged to the affluent Rajvansh family, the business tycoons but he was down to earth and never showed off his money or status and that was what I loved about him. He dropped in home often to drop Ana if they were late and sat on the floor to eat with us. He said he loved the simple food I cooked more than what the army of butlers in his mansion made.

He was a charmer and I knew these were all his talks to show that he didn't find a difference in class or status among us and he actually didn't. He had asked me politely if he should talk to his elder brother and pay the hospital bills, when mom and dad were in the hospital and I had blanched at his words. He had cared and he knew our reality. I wasn't working at that time either, I was studying too.

"No way!" Had been my stunned reply and he had backed off not uttering another money word, but I knew he was always on the lookout for Ana and my safety and if we needed anything. I had never met anyone from his family but was sure they would all be warm people given how good he was.

I didn't have any friends like Ana had her little close circle. I would have probably had them if I didn't have to rush off to find a job and not go back to college for post-graduation. All my friends from school and college days had gone on to study more and made a better life for themselves than the rut I was currently in. But their situation was not the same as mine and I had nothing to complain about. It was my decision to leave my dreams behind and work, even though I had had no choice back then, nor did I have one now.

I finished my graduation in business administration three years ago but was yet to find a decent job that would pay after the company I had been working in for the past two years closed down. It had been more than six months since and I was still on the lookout for a well-paying job. Last to last year, my boss had urged me to pursue my dream of fashion design and got me enrolled in part-time classes while I worked full-time at their office.

Now, with my final exams approaching, it was difficult to manage two jobs, studying, and household chores all at once. But I knew I had to do this. This course could open up newer avenues of jobs and options for me. It could get me a better paying job and I would not have to struggle so much to let Ana finish her college. I had buried my dreams of post-graduation but I wouldn't let her follow in my footsteps.

She would do her post-graduation after completing her graduation next year and I had already started saving for that. As I was learning to design, my teacher felt I was gifted and she helped me sell two of my designs to one of the designers' boutique companies as well. They didn't pay me much, but something was always better than nothing.

I sighed, pulled my books out of my tote bag, and glanced around the library. It seemed like a quiet day today and I could only see a handful of students sitting in a corner actually reading from the books they had laid out in front of them and I couldn't see any shadows behind the shelves of students making out in the library. Oh yeah, that happened all the time and I had to walk in parallel shelves making noise to get them to detangle and rush out of the library or go their different ways.

I buried my head in my book, learning the various concepts used in fashion design and practiced my designs.

"Excuse me!"

"Yes!" I looked up from my design to see a final year student peering down at me.

"I can't find M.L.Seth Macro Economics, can you check if it has been checked out by anyone?"

"Give me one sec!"

It was such a rhetorical question, obviously the book was checked out or borrowed by someone if he couldn't find it in its shelf, but then some people just needed to show that they were thorough and needed the book.

"Yes, it should be back on Thursday! So probably come back and check on Friday!"

"What time Thursday?"

"How do I know?" I rolled my eyes at the idiotic question. How would I know what time on Thursday the student who had borrowed would turn up to return the book?

"Fine!"

He walked out of the library; no, he stomped out of the library as if annoyed with my response. He must be a spoilt rich brat who was always served everything on a silver platter.

I locked up the library at sharp 4:30 in the evening as I had to rush over to the pharmacy, where I had my second job. I sat at the pharmacy shop and attended from 5 PM to 9 PM until the shop owner returned at 9 to take over and sit for the entire night. The pharmacy was only about two kilometers from my house and on the main busy market street. It was managed by a family and in the evening, they needed one more person to manage the shop so the family could meet for at least a few hours at home. I was more than happy to pitch in as they paid me a decent amount for the four hours and if the rush was less then I managed to study in the shop too.

I parked my *Activa,* outside the pharmacy shop and was surprised when the lady of the shop greeted me.

"Hello, Aunty!"

"Trisha Beta, good you came, I was waiting for you!"

"Sorry aunty, there was a lot of traffic on the way. How come you are here today?"

"Manik has gone to Surat for three days, so I and Meena were here all day."

I smiled. The family members were all warm and nice, another reason why I had approached them for this part time work and they all treated me well, trusting their shop and the cash box with me for a few hours.

"I will be making *Puranpoli* tomorrow, shall I send for you?" *Puranpoli* was a sweet delicacy made of gram flour bread filled with delicious dal, and coconut filling. My mouth watered at her offer.

"Oh, Aunty!" I smiled at her, touched that she thought of me. When mom was alive, she often made it for us. Though it was not very difficult nor time-consuming, in the mad rush that I lived currently, I had never even attempted to make it for me and Ana after Mom.

"I know you and your sister love it."

"We do! Thank you, Aunty!"

"God bless you *beta!*" She patted my shoulder and walked away. I settled on the comfortable chair behind the counter and took my sketchbook out.

"That's stunning!" I was startled by the voice. I was so lost in my sketch that I did not realize a customer stood right opposite me.

"Sorry!" I looked up to find dark brown enchanting eyes looking down at me. The stranger was tall and oh so handsome! He had a handsome face, which personified calm. One glance at him and I felt that he was Mr. Dependable of every group he would have been a part of.

"I needed aspirins, Dolo, one vitamin B over-the-counter strip, and..." He paused trying to remember then raised his finger as he dialled a number.

I turned around to pick out the medicines he had already asked for, while his call connected.

"Hey Shlok, Aspirins, Dolo, and what else was it that you needed?"

He paused and winced looking up at me.

"Shit man! You should buy it for yourself!"

He cut the call and looked uneasily at me.

"I also need..." he was hesitant and looked around. Why would a guy be hesitant to ask for a medicine, I wondered and then it dawned on me.

"This?" I pointed to the shelf that displayed several condoms.

"Shit, yes, 1 pack please! And a lube."

"Which one?"

"I don't know, just any super thin one!"

I packed up his items and gave him the bill, he made an online payment and collected his packet.

"That is not for me! My friend..." He frowned, "Why am I telling you this!"

I burst into laughter, unable to control it any longer and he joined in too as he shook his head and turned to walk back to his parked car.

He was so cute!

And handsome!

# CHAPTER TWO

# LITTLE SUNSHINE

*Trisha*

"Who was he?" Ana looked at me baffled.

"I don't know, done with college?"

"Yes! I came to give you this, Yuvi is waiting I am going home, now." She passed me a small parcel of food and I snatched it hungrily.

Masala Idlis!

"Thanks!"

I looked behind her at Yuvraj, who sat on his bike, waiting for Ana and waved at me. I waved back.

"Tell na, who was he, why were you both laughing?"

"I don't know he came here to buy condoms for his friend and was super embarrassed about it and started explaining that those weren't for him but for his friend."

"He was trying to make an impression!"

"Nothing like that, he seemed like a shy guy."

"And he was so tall!"

"Yeah, and handsome!" I giggled.

"Oh shoot, I didn't see his face!" Ana pouted and I burst into laughter yet again.

I picked a small piece of Masala Idli and shoved it in her mouth and she grinned.

"Not fair!" Yuvraj yelled from his bike.

I stepped out of the shop with another piece in my hand and fed him too.

"You are the best!" He blew me a kiss and I laughed as both of them went off.

It was an unusually busy day at the shop and I was bone tired by the time I got back home at 9:15. Luckily, dad was not at home and Ana was studying in peace.

"Trish, I soaked rice, I was thinking just make pulao today!"

"Are you sure, yesterday also we ate rice at night."

"It's okay. He isn't here anyway!"

"Never know he will come!" I sighed as I sat down to chop veggies for pulao and then an idea struck me, why eat boring pulao when we could eat fried rice. I shooed Ana out of the kitchen and quickly put rice for cooking on one stove and started stir-frying the veggies on another. Ana loved fried rice and she would be delighted to see the menu change.

She was my little sunshine in an otherwise boring life. Past few years, since mom expired, we both had become each other's lifeline. I had to grow up and shoulder responsibilities as I saw my father plunge into darkness.

Now, my dad had no job and didn't even try to work, all he did was drink all day long and come home only to take his frustration out on either of us. Every night was a struggle when he would come home, either he would be so drunk that someone would drop him at the door, or if he would be in his senses then his demands would begin.

"Why is there no chicken?"

"Why have you made rice for dinner?"

"I want a proper meal? Why is there only one sabzi?"

There was no point telling him that earning to have food ready was also a challenge. He would often hit me for just the absence of salt or absence of taste buds in his vile mouth. He would throw up and then we would need to clean that mess too.

Ana and I prayed and hoped some nights when we were too exhausted for him to not return at all. And that happened once in a while, we would have no clue where he would spend the night, but sometimes he would just not return and we would sleep in peace that night.

It was almost midnight when I lay down on the bed and Ana snuggled up to me.

"I miss her, di!"

Ana only ever called me Di when she was emotional. She was four years younger than me but she always called me by my name.

I turned to face her and she lifted her eyes slowly to meet my gaze.

"I miss her too!" I whispered. "But am sure, she is at peace now!"

"I hope so, and I hope she is not looking down at us."

"Why?"

"Because then she would see our plight and would never be at peace."

"True!" I paused, "But she would also be proud of us, right? At least a little?"

"She would be super proud of you, Di, and a little proud of Deeksha Di and me!"

"Why a little?"

"Let's be honest, Deeksha Di and I aren't really doing anything outside of the basic that is expected of us, Mom wouldn't have let you take on all the responsibilities and would have scolded us if we both took advantage of your big heart!"

I laughed at her words.

"Deeksha is managing her house, her husband, in-laws everything, she is settled and doing good. You are doing wonderfully well in college and studying so well, of course Maa would be proud of you both! I don't even have a proper job and am shuffling between these useless jobs!"

"But Di..." She left her words hanging.

We both knew my jobs were not at all useless, they were enabling us to have the basics we needed and meals in our tummy. I pulled her in my arms and we both fell asleep snuggling together.

Deeksha was four years older than me while Anaisha was four years younger. We three had been very close all our lives and spoke every day. Our father always resented that he didn't have a son, a typical want of a male child and he had taken to alcohol quite early on. Mom till she was there had shielded us girls well and kept us locked inside the room, whenever he returned home drunk, which was only occasionally.

The house we lived in was a small one-bedroom apartment on the ground floor of an old building, but it was our own, and not a rented apartment. That was the biggest relief. I only had to struggle to buy us food, pay college fees and make sure we had clothes and basics. I never had to worry that we might not have a roof over our heads.

I had just come to the pharmacy and settled down when my phone rang.

"Hello?"

"Hey Babes! Miss me?"

"Alok, when did you come back?"

"Today early morning, couldn't sleep on the flight, so was sleeping, free tonight?"

"Tonight? No, you know how hectic my weekdays are, can we meet this weekend?"

"Of course, let me plan something for the weekend. How have you been?"

"I missed you!"

"I missed you too, but this trip was important and you know I was with my dad, so I couldn't even call you!"

"Yeah, I know!"

"I got something for you!"

"What?"

"Nope, not telling you. I want to see your expression when you see it, let's plan to go to my bachelor pad this weekend."

"Alok!"

"Please, that's safest if we don't want to bump into anyone and you know I can behave!"

"I know!"

"Okay then I got to go, you take good care of my girlfriend! And I will see you on Saturday."

"You too take care, Love you!"

"Love you babes!"

I stared at my phone long after I had disconnected the call. That was Alok, my boyfriend of the past four years. He was a senior in my college and had pursued me relentlessly till I gave in. He belonged to an elite family and I had my apprehensions but as they say, love won at the end and we were going steady now.

Since a year and half, he had started helping out with his family business and he was out with his father on a work trip for the past three weeks. Whenever he travelled, he barely ever called, he only messaged me at odd times. When he was here, we tried to sneak out to meet on the weekends, because weekdays were super hectic for me, with my two jobs, studies, and everything else.

"Trish, see this!" Ana came over to me with her phone in her hand.

Another cute cat reel, I was sure!

"Rajvansh Textiles is looking for intern designers for the upcoming garments business, they have ventured into. Why don't you apply?"

"But I don't even have the course diploma yet!"

"So, what, they are asking for CV and designs to shortlist for interview. You can clarify that your exams are coming up in three weeks and you would then have the diploma."

"Really? Why would they consider someone without even a diploma, when so many bigger designers would apply and scramble for this job!"

"What is the harm in applying?"

"Hmmm..." I remained non-committal. Rajvansh Textiles was huge and it was like a lifetime dream to get a chance to work with them.

"Actually, I can ask Yuvi to refer you, I think his brother handles textiles, or maybe his uncle, I can check."

"No!"

"Why not? He can talk to them, and get the interview arranged, after that is all on you!"

"No! I would never take that kind of help from Yuvraj!"

"What kind of help?"

We both froze as Yuvraj's voice sounded right behind me.

"Nothing!" I said and glared at Ana.

"What?" He looked between us sisters.

"How are you?" I smiled at him.

"Ana!"

"Trish is not ready to take your help for arranging an interview in Rajvansh Textiles." Ana blurted and I looked at her shocked.

Yuvraj started laughing.

"Trisha doesn't need my help at all, apply and send your designs am sure they will take a look and hire you! Moreover, Bhai handles textiles, if I said a word, he would not just kick me but he would also not hire her."

"Huh?" Ana's jaw dropped open.

"Yeah, he believes in hard work and merit, not in recommendations." He grinned at Ana, then turned to me, "Please apply, I have seen your designs they are good. I know Bhai will like them."

I nodded just to get the two off my case but I was not too sure if I wanted to apply and face rejection so early in my career, well what career, I had not even finished my exams. Then I remembered what my mom used to say often – *'If you don't try, you have already failed!'*

I didn't want to fail; I didn't want to regret later either so I decided to try and remain pragmatic about it. I would just apply for the experience of it, and won't lose hope if they didn't shortlist me, which was highly likely.

I was in the kitchen preparing dinner when the main door burst open and Dad stumbled in. He threw in the empty bottle, making it crash against the wall. Damn, the mess and the glass shards to clean now. I was bone tired, my exams were round the corner and the studies along with everything else were taking a toll on my sanity.

"He is drunk!" Ana whispered and I nodded at her.

She was scared of the times Dad got into a fitful rage after drinking too much. I was scared too but being the elder one among the two of us, I couldn't show my vulnerability. I had to stand up for both of us, I had to shield her and take his wrath every single time. Dad was angry at the world, angry at himself, at us, and most of all our mom for dying from his mistake!

"Go inside." I whispered.

"No, we will both be here!"

"Where is my dinner?" Dad yelled, making something flip inside me. I was so done with these daily tantrums.

I switched the stove off and walked out to face him.

"Freshen up, dinner is getting ready!" I said keeping my voice steady, not showing the fear I felt within.

"Why is it not ready, yet?"

"Because it takes time to cook. I can serve raw *dal* and rice if you want."

He raised his hand to hit me and Ana took in a sharp breath but I had had enough and I grabbed his hand before he could hit me. He had lost weight in past few years and was frail now, barely able to stand straight in his current drunken state.

"Wash your hands and face if you want any food!" I glared back at him.

"How dare you?" He yelled at me.

"I will, I earn, I buy the grocery, I cook. You want food, stop yelling and clean up!" I yelled back.
He took a step back shocked, because this was the first time, I had blocked his blow or answered him back that too in a raised voice. He shook his head but walked inside.

"Di?"

"It's okay, go inside and study. I will call when dinner is ready, don't come in front of him." I patted her cheek and Ana rushed inside worried.

I was worried too; it was the first time I had answered back and I didn't know what more was in store for me. Dad was very unpredictable when he was drunk, which he was all the time these days. The guilt that mom died because of him, because of his drinking had eaten him up inside, but instead of sobering up, he had plunged further into the darkness and taken shelter in the lap of alcohol.

# CHAPTER THREE

# FINDING HER

*Viraj Rajvansh*

The beats of the music filled not just the car but the podium and the lawn as well. I walked out of my house to find Shlok waiting in his car for me.

"Naman ditched us again!" He grunted.

"Why?"

"He is busy with a new case!"

"Damn, you told him we are going to Rave?"

"Yes! And still he declined saying the case was crucial."

"Okay, let's go!"

"I have run out of my supplies and would need to stop on our way!"

"Again?"

"Man! Those are meant to be used."

I just shook my head as I walked around the car to get in the passenger seat, Shlok was a man-whore. Every night he slept with someone different and there was no stopping him. He got a thrill out of it. Naman and I had sobered down quite a bit since our crazy college days, well Naman was never as crazy as us anyway.

Even I had sobered down and I often went back home alone now, but Shlok, never. He had another apartment just for this. Like me Shlok too lived with his parents in their house. Mine was a big joint family while his was not.

Naman was the first one in our trio to purchase a flat of his own, a lavish penthouse and he had set it up too, living there sometimes and living with his dad at times. His mom died when he was just a few days old, some complications in delivery he had once gruntled and he was close to his dad. They both were each other's rock unlike me and my dad.

Shlok also loved his dad and would do just about anything his old man would ask of him but not me. I rarely saw eye to eye with my dad, more so since I took over the CEO role in Rajvansh industries. My dad was not in favour of me taking the throne yet, he wanted me to prove myself and I took up the challenge. I not only proved myself I outdid his performance too and ascended the CEO post as per our agreement. Since then, the distance between me and my dad had slowly and steadily been increasing, so much so that now we barely spoke to each other and were only civil when we had an audience. When alone, we both chose silence over any words.

My mom worshipped the ground her husband walked on and rarely ever said a word against him. She chastised me often for being the disgruntled son and not behaving properly with my dad who had ensured I was at the position I currently was at. My younger brother Yuvraj was the apple of my eye, my baby. He was seven years younger than me, and there was nothing that I wouldn't do for him. I also had a little sister, when I was four years old, but she was born prematurely and couldn't survive for long. She was about a week old when she breathed her last leaving my mom completely devastated and depressed. For a couple of years, my aunt, Rashmi Kaki, Vikash uncle's wife took care of me until my mom got pregnant again and gave birth to Yuvraj.

I think that was the time when I learnt to live on my own and the initial distance between me and my parents began to form. My dad also neglected me as he took care of my mom, while mom was too depressed to realize that though she had lost her daughter, her son was still too young and needed her as much.

To date I love Rashmi Kaki the most, for she was the one who stepped in and took care of me, completely devoting herself to my care alongside her son Rohit and her daughter Vandana. I was close to both my cousins and my brother alike. Vandana was our little princess, too spoilt yet a darling. Rohit was just a year younger than me and now helped me with the management of the company. He was the finance guy of our family and had taken up the CFO position last year when I took up the CEO role.

"Viraj?" Rashmi Kaki's voice stopped me from shutting the car door and I stepped out. "Will you be back for dinner?"

"No Kaki, we will have dinner outside."

"But you will come home at night, right?"

"Of course, Kaki, is something wrong?"

"No, I just wanted to check whether to wait for you or not."

"I will come home, for sure, but please don't wait for me, Kaki. You know I don't like it!"

"A mother can't sleep in peace till she knows where her child is!" She smiled, her love for me shining through her old eyes. She had aged beautifully and gracefully in all these years.

"Some can!" I snapped and sat back in the car, wincing immediately realizing I took out the anger of my mom on her.

Shlok put the car in gear and I saw Kaki standing waving at me in the rear-view mirror. I would apologize to her tomorrow morning, first thing, I decided.

"Dude, I need to stop here, do you want anything?" Shlok asked as he parked the car on the roadside.

My phone rang and I picked it up, it was from Naman. I gestured for Shlok to walk ahead while I spoke to Naman. I had asked him to look at some of the legal papers for a new partnership I wanted to start under the Rajvansh group of industries. I spoke for a few minutes and turned around to enter the pharmacy shop, where Shlok had gone in.

I froze at the vision in front of me, as I stepped inside the shop. Shlok stood choosing a pack of condoms from some ten that were in front of him at the counter. On the other side of the counter was the girl I had been searching for, for the past six months now. The girl I had seen a glimpse of in Yuvraj's college and though I went back to his college several times after that on some pretext or other but never managed to catch her glimpse.

"*Anamika!*" I whispered as I walked up to the counter. That was the name I had given her in my mind. I couldn't believe she was standing in front of me, in flesh and blood, after all these months of searching.

She looked up at me and I was struck by a thunderbolt. Her dark grey eyes settled on me as they studied my face. The depth of the eyes pulled me into a whirlpool of varied feelings. I felt a flutter where my heart was supposed to be and I felt something like a fire, spark and take hold of me as I held her gaze. Her lips parted to say something but no sound came out.

I slowly moved my gaze down from her face and her long neck came into view, she wore a maroon-coloured top or maybe a Kurta which had a V-shaped neckline and covered the rest of her body from my scrutiny. Her ears had round, beautiful silver *Jhumkas*, I guessed that was what they were called and after the new song, they were a fashion rage, I supposed.

I couldn't see her hair; I remembered a long plait from the previous encounter and wondered if they were still as long or had she cut them off. How I hoped, she had not, and she still carried those long tresses, but there was no way for me to check that now, unless I looked like a certified pervert going behind the counter to check her out.

"Dude, which one do you want?"

"Huh?" I turned to Shlok; he was asking me something.

"Which one, flavoured, thin, super thin, intense?"

"Anything! I mean nothing!" I blurted looking at her, her gaze was still locked with me but it was getting angry by the minute for some reason.

Did she recognize me?

No, not possible, it had been more than six months now.

Why was she angry at me?

"Moron!" Shlok threw a pack at me and I impulsively caught it. "How much for these two?"

She turned her icy glare at Shlok and gave him the bill. He made the payment and walked out of the shop while I stood rooted in my spot, holding the pack of condom that Shlok had thrown at me, like an idiot.

"What? You wanted anything else?"

I turned to look at him and sighed. I couldn't let him know anything or else he would meddle in my matter. I loved him like my brother but in her case, I didn't want any meddling, that was the reason I hadn't asked Naman to find anything about her. I had kept searching for her on my own. She was my little secret, my little desire, my obsession and my *Anamika*. I shook my head turned around and settled in his car.

"I don't want this!" I threw the pack back at him and he caught it, before putting the car in gear.

"Why? Dry spell?"

"Yeah!" I looked back at her, one last time before the car merged into traffic and I lost sight of her in the mirror.

"That's why we are going to Rave, you can break your dry spell."

"No, I don't want to."

"Excuse me?"

"Nothing, I have to get back home and apologize to Kaki, I was very rude earlier."

"Shut up man, stop talking about Kaki when I am talking about hot, young chicks!"

I groaned; this man would probably never change.

After seeing her yet again, I was in no mood to go to Rave, I just wanted to sit at the pharmacy shop and stare at her. I could as well setup a camp and settle in front of her.

Six months back when I had not seen her during the college fest, I had gone to the campus for three weeks in a row on some pretext or another to just be able to catch a glimpse of her but I had failed miserably. Not once, had I been able to see her. out of desperation, I had even bribed a clerk to find information about the dance teacher and to my utter dismay he told me, there was no dance teacher at all in the college, she must have been some student, who was probably better than others and hence had taken up teaching the steps. My hopes were shattered but there wasn't much I could do.

I had been so tempted to turn to Naman to help me find her, but I had no name, no photo to go on. I saw her in my dreams every single night, so one night I drew up her sketch, which gave me satisfaction and happiness like nothing else had. She soon became my muse and I designed the entire collection thinking of her.

At nights, when I couldn't fall asleep, I took to sketching her face, her features out. I kept the sketches well hidden in my closet because if anyone glanced at them, I was in for trouble. I had no answers for why I was so obsessed with her when I had beauty all around me. I had no dearth of girls dying to be my girlfriend, my one-night stands, or anything in between but I had no interest in any of them. I was interested in this one girl, whom I knew nothing about until today.

Today I learned that she worked here at the pharmacy, now I could see her and find out more about her. All thanks to Shlok and his never-ending need to buy condoms! I knew instantly what I was going to sketch tonight, those pretty ears with those silver *jhumkas*. I was mesmerized with her all over again! Her grey eyes fueled my obsession yet again making me want to make her mine. No other girl would ever match up to her, and I wanted none if not her.

"Thanks, Man!" I muttered as we got out of the car to step into the nightclub.

"Thanks for?" He frowned.

"Hasn't it been long since we came here?"

"We have not even stepped inside!" He laughed and I smiled, unable to tell him, what I was thanking him truly for.

I wrapped up my work as early as I could and rushed out of the office at 7 only to get stuck in Mumbai traffic. I was not headed home tonight; I was headed to see my only obsession. I was headed towards the pharmacy store to get a glimpse of her.

As the traffic cleared and I inched towards her shop, I noticed several people standing waiting at the counter. I slowly parked the car, across the street and sat in it watching until the throng of people cleared and I saw her sigh and settle on the chair behind the counter and pull out a book to read.

Today she wore a dark blue-coloured t-shirt with some graphics on the front. Her hair was tied behind in a ponytail and she looked like a young college student. My heart dropped again, was she Yuvraj's classmate, was I stalking a child?

Then I shook my head, no, she was no child, she was a beautiful young woman. A woman who had stolen my peace, she was a thief and she sat there oblivious to the turmoil she put me through for the past few months.

Several college students worked part time jobs to help pay for their fees or education loans, and if that was the case with her, I could help her too. But for that I needed to talk to her, know more about her. Yesterday I had lost my voice at her mere sight, I wondered if I should approach her now that she was alone in the shop or maybe not, she was so young, she might get scared if I approached and could take my intentions in a wrong way.

It was dark and yet she looked unfazed as an elderly man joined her in the shop, she chatted with him, showed him something in a book, probably the register of transactions, and then stepped out. I straightened in my seat as she walked to a parked bike on the curb. She started it, waved at the elderly man in the shop, and zoomed into the traffic. She was tall and the way she balanced the bike easily made something flutter within me.

It had been four days since I came here to watch her for hours at a stretch from across the street and every night at about 9-9:15 she left on her *Activa* to go back home. I had even memorized the model, colour and number of her bike. Today I was determined to follow her and see where she lived. I think she had noticed my car in the past few days but she never bothered to look closely. She turned and glanced once towards my car as she started her *Activa* today and rode on.

She stood at a signal waiting for it to turn green when her gaze fell on my car in her rear-view mirror and I noticed her stiffening. But she didn't turn to look who was in the car, as the signal turned green, she just drove on at normal speed not showing whether she was bothered about being followed or not. After a few minutes, she turned into a narrow lane, it was dark and lonely in the lane but I didn't turn behind her, I stopped at the curb watching her until she parked her *Activa* inside a small building on the left side of the road.

So, this was where she lived, this was an old neighbourhood and not a very good or safe locality. My heart flipped at the thought that she lived here and travelled home alone at night. I wondered who was at her home. I wondered what I could do to ensure that she stayed safe even in this area. I could put guards to trail her but then my family could find out about it and she might get scared seeing the guards. I had no right to do that when she didn't have any idea of my existence.

So, it was up to me to keep her safe for the time being!

For more than two weeks I stalked her and saw her get into the ground floor apartment after parking her bike outside, it was a Thursday evening when I was as usual following her until she turned in the lane and stopped abruptly. I stopped my car to see three guys were blocking her way. I sat still watching until one of them raised his hand to touch her face and she flinched back.

I was out of my car within a second and one of the boys saw me. He was tall and directly faced me, he watched me as I walked closer to them.

"What's going on here?" I called out.

They all took a step back and she looked nervously at me. Our gaze met and for the first time I saw slight worry in her eyes. I didn't like that look of fear or was it anxiety in her eyes.

"You go on!" I told her but she stood staring at me.

I paused in my tracks and kept watching her as no one moved. She flinched when one guy tried to touch her hand again and turned to kick him in the shins, before he could move, her knee landed on his groin and he fell back on the ground shrieking in pain.

Good job, *Anamika*! That's my brave girl!

The other two guys looked at him and stepped forward to grab her. By then I had walked up to her and while she kicked the shorter guy, I punched the taller one in his face to make him stumble back.

"You leave!" I said again and this time, she got on her bike and drove away to her house.

Once I saw she was away and safe, I attacked the three guys raining blows and punches without bothering to see who got hurt where. The guy she had landed on the ground also tried to get up but I kicked him down again. The three of them all were down on the ground and bleeding profusely at several places from all the rough handling they had been dealt with, in the span of last five minutes.

I grabbed the collar of the tall guy, I had hit in the face, blood trickling from his nose and mouth and pulled him close to me.

"You or anyone in this area looks at her again and I won't leave you in a state to be able to look at anyone anymore!" He shuddered at my chilling warning. "This was nothing, you won't have hands to touch any girl or eyes to even see your own family!"

"We meant no harm!"

"Good! What about these two?"

"We will not trouble her!"

"Good."

The shorter guy tried to stand up slowly.

"Who are you?"

"Doesn't matter. But if you or anyone else bothers her, you all will find out who I am. And trust me you all won't like it."

I nodded at them to leave and they ran off in the opposite direction.

# CHAPTER FOUR

# Dream Come True

*Viraj*

"Bhai, I don't know if I want to join Rajvansh Industries at all!" Yuvraj announced before he plopped down on my bed.

I was getting ready for office when he walked in looking sleepy, as if he was sleepwalking and made his grand announcement.

"Yuvi? What happened?" I frowned wondering if he knew he was on my bed right now.

"None of my friends would be with me!"

I chuckled.

"We can give them all a job!"

"Can we?" He sat up straight his eyes glistening eagerly. He had been wanting to refer someone, I understood.

"If they are any good!"

"Bhai, I thought you were against any references!"

"Yes, I am. But for you, I would do anything, you must know that."

"If that is the case, there is a new designer, she is learning, but I want you to see her designs!"

"Interesting! Who is she?"

"My friend's sister! Have you met Anaisha?"

I frowned; I was hearing a girl's name for the first time from him.

"No, I don't think so!"

"Oh, okay!" He paused.

"So, this girl Anaisha is learning fashion designing?"

"No, her sister and she is too good! Pure talent."

I shook my head, pure talent, yeah right! Just then I heard a knock on the door and Rohit walked in.

"Viraj!" He paused when he saw Yuvi in my room, "Am I disturbing?"

"Not at all, come!"

"I wanted your signature on this document and I was wondering if we could go to office together, I wanted to pick your brain on this new incentive I have been thinking about."

"Sure, let's go. I am ready!" I took the document from him and glanced over it before signing and returning it to him.

"But Bhai!"

"Let's talk in the evening, Yuvi!" I called back as I stepped out of my bedroom with Rohit.

I rubbed my hands over my face, I was tired, I had back-to-back meetings all day today and I had not even eaten any lunch. I looked at the watch it was 4:00 already, too late for lunch. But I wanted to step out of my cabin and stretch my legs. I decided to walk up to the pantry and get myself some coffee.

"Viraj, you need something?" My assistant Rajni got up as she saw me walking out.

"Sit, I need a coffee."

"I will bring it."

"No, I need to walk as well, I will take it."

I gestured for her to sit down and walked ahead. Pantry was on the floor below mine and I climbed down the stairs instead of taking the elevator. My phone rang and I paused to see who it was.

"Hello, Shlok!"

"Dude, dinner tonight!"

"No, I will be late tonight."

"What is keeping you so busy, every evening neither are you available nor are you in the office!" I winced he was catching on. I couldn't tell him where I was every evening.

I raked my brain to think of a good reason but nothing that could satisfy his eagerness came to mind. I looked up and there she stood, dressed smartly in a dark grey trouser suit and a mint green shirt. Wow! She looked so beautiful and professional in this attire, perfect for work. Then I paused, I had started hallucinating too. I rubbed my eyes and looked again, yes, she was still there.

"I will call you back!" I told Shlok and cut the call, as I walked towards where she stood at the reception.

Jyoti, our HR head walked in just then and I held her elbow.

"Who is that?" I asked pointing at my obsession.

"She is a fashion designer, she is learning, her exam results are not out yet, but she applied for the vacancy we have and her designs look mind blowing to me, so I asked her to come and go through a round of interviews."

My heart flipped in my heart.

She was a fashion designer; my mind went into an overdrive scheming on ideas to hire her and keep her close to me.

"Show me!" I said as I turned my focus on Jyoti.

I looked at her CV.

**Trisha Agarwal**

Trisha!

What a lovely name! I repeated it several times in my head. Almost seven months later, now I knew her name. I scanned through her CV and then turned the sheet over to look at the designs she had submitted and actually as Jyoti said they were mind blowing.

"Send her to my cabin. I will talk to her!"

"But Viraj?"

"Yeah, send her upstairs." I turned back to go back to my cabin, "Jyoti?"

"Yes, Viraj."

"Can you also ask someone to bring two cups of coffee to my cabin?"

"Two cups?"

"Yeah, why not! I need coffee desperately."

"Sure!" She frowned but walked towards where my angel stood.

So, *Anamika* finally had a name - Trisha! I chuckled.

I stood gazing out of the window behind my desk at the sprawling sea at a distance when there was a brief knock on the door and I heard Jyoti's voice.

"Viraj?"

I turned around and she took a step back horrified as I stalked towards her slowly.

"This is Trisha, here for the interview." I nodded. "Trisha, this is our CEO and Chief Designer, Viraj Rajvansh!"

I extended my hand towards her and she looked at it for a few seconds before putting her soft hand in mine. A bolt of electricity ran through my body at the slight contact. Her fingers were icy cold and she pulled her hand back.

"Thanks Jyoti!" I looked at our HR head to leave. "Please sit Ms. Trisha!"

I gestured for her to sit down while I moved back to take my chair. She sat down slowly and pushed her CV and designs towards me.

"I saw these. So, tell me about yourself."

Before she could say anything, there was a knock on the door and I grunted my displeasure.

"Come in!"

"Sir, you asked for coffee?"

"Yes, please leave it here! Thank you!" I dismissed the office boy. I went around and kept one cup in front of her.

"No, Sir!"

"You don't drink coffee?"

"I do." I leaned down and she moved back in her chair.

"Then?"

"Now? I am fine. Thanks!" She shook her head.

Her sensuous lips trembled and I wanted to take them between mine and show them how much I liked their sweetness. I chastised myself, what the heck was I thinking of in my office. She was here for the first time, and I needed her to come here everyday going forward. I needed to step back.

"Relax, have some, else I will have to drink alone." I came around the desk to put some distance between us. "Go on, tell me about yourself!"

I took a sip of coffee and it tasted so much better just because I was sharing it with her. She took a small sip too and then she started narrating about her college degree, courses she had done, and her job experience. I pulled the CV closer to check she passed out of college 3 years ago, so she was not as young as I had thought. I relaxed a bit and focused back on her words. Her voice was soft and soothing my soul. After seven months of craving to hear her talk, craving to see her up close, I didn't know what to ask her, what to say. I somehow found myself tongue tied which was rare.

She looked at me after finishing her introduction, waiting for the next question.

"So why are you working at the pharmacy?" Her hands shook nervously.

"Sir, the company as I mentioned closed down six months back and since then I am looking for a job but nothing worked out. So?"

"So, you will work at a pharmacy?"

"Sir, something is better than nothing in my world. That few hours job pays me money to buy groceries for the house."

"Few hours? What else do you do with the rest of your time?"

"Sir, I am working as the Librarian at the college I passed out of. And was studying too, finished my exams last week."

I frowned and looked at her CV. She was working as a Librarian in Yuvi's college. No wonder!

"Are you married?"

"Sir?"

"It's not mentioned here!"

She gulped then slowly shook her head.

"When can you join work?"

"Join? Ahh, next week?"

"Okay, you are hired. I will ask Jyoti to send your offer letter. Any particular salary you have in mind?"

She looked at me confused then slowly shook her head. She had no idea what this job could pay her. I was sure she came from a poor family background and had responsibilities on her shoulders. I so wanted to find out who all was in her family but asking her today would be crossing a line.

"Congratulations!" I stood up and extended my hand toward her. She shook it lightly and turned to leave. She paused at the door and turned back.

"Sir, can I ask something?"

"Call me Viraj, everyone else does."

"Viraj? Can I ask something?" My name sounded so good on her shaky, soft voice and I wondered how it would feel if she screamed my name in throes of passion. Then I shook my head I was racing ahead of myself.

"Yes, go on!"

"Why?" She looked up and our gaze met, "Why do you follow me every night?"

I kept looking at her, she was nervous, no she was confused, she was not nervous, she was just baffled by today's encounter.

"Have those guys troubled you again?"

"No!" She shook her head.

"Do you want me to not follow you?"

"Yes!"

"Yes, to follow you or not follow you?"

"Not follow me!"

I closed my eyes.

"I will try!"

She stayed quiet but her expressive eyes showed she had a thousand questions running in her head.

I grinned to myself as she left and closed the door behind her. I picked up the phone and dialled my HR head.

"Jyoti, hire this girl and make her my assistant designer. She will work for me, directly!"

"For you? But that is not how..."

"Yeah, not everyone but she will!" My tone was curt and she got the message. She was mistaken if she thought I would explain or change my stand.

"Okay, and anything else?"

"Send her the offer letter, joining sometime next week, and yeah pay her good."

"Okay! But she doesn't even have her diploma yet!"

"She will get it. She is good, I will make her the best!"

"Is something going on Viraj?"

"What do you mean?" My voice sharp all of sudden.

"Nothing, I will send her the offer letter right away."

"Thanks Jyoti!"

I put the phone down.

Finally, after seven months, I will get to see her every day, and I will get to work with her every day.

My heart soared in anticipation of the coming months and calm fell over my mind when I realized my obsession with her would now bring fruit and I had a chance to see her outside of my hallucinations and dreams.

My muse would work with me now!

# CHAPTER FIVE

# TURN OF EVENTS

*Trisha*

I thought it was surreal that my profile was shortlisted for the initial round of interview by Rajvansh Textiles but what followed next was by far the most unimaginable incident of my life.

I stepped out of the Rajvansh Industries building and just sat on the bench outside to breathe. To just soak in what I had experienced.

The CEO of the Rajvansh industry himself interviewed me.

My designs were liked by Yuvraj's brother Viraj Rajvansh.

I was hired by my stalker himself.

And best of all, or maybe the worst was that all these were just one guy, the guy who had showed up at my pharmacy and then started stalking me every day.

I know he sat in his fancy car across the street watching me for hours. That perturbed me but I kept myself calm all these days, he was no threat if he was across the street and I didn't want to talk to him and give him any importance that what he did was impacting me in any way.

But then he started following me back home too, that was scary, super scary. Why the hell was he following me every day to watch me get home? Today, when I asked, he said he would try not to stalk, what was that supposed to mean!

The day after those boys stopped me in the street, they had all come to apologize heavily bandaged and a chill ran down my spine realizing he had beaten them up single-handedly after I left.

Who was he?

What did he want from me?

And today in the office, he was so gentle. Offering me coffee, speaking to me softly, and then just like that he offered me a job.

Did I get the job because of my designs or because he seemed obsessed with me?

Could I even take the job? What would he do if I worked with him every day?

I wished I had someone I could confide in, but I couldn't talk about this to Ana, she was naïve and would romanticize all this and I definitely couldn't mention to Alok, he would blow his fuse and would not let me work at Rajvansh textiles, which in itself was a wonderful opportunity.

I could call Deeksha Di and maybe ask her to meet me once and share, she would surely be able to guide. I pulled my phone out of my bag and noticed there was an email. I opened the mail and it was the offer letter, he had promised.

Joining from next week, Friday and then my gaze fell on the renumeration and the phone almost slipped off my hands. I clutched it tighter and read the number again. Will they pay me this much? The salary meant I could clear off the education loan I had taken for Ana within 3 months and if I continued working for a year or so, I would have saved enough to get Ana to do her master's too. My decision was made in a minute. I needed the money; I needed the job.

So, what if he was my stalker, he hadn't crossed any line and I just hoped he wouldn't in office too. Obviously, he wouldn't. He was the CEO of a family held company; he would try and stay clear of a scandal. I would keep my head low and work, I would learn and I would maintain my distance. He was well behaved and gentle in the office today.

Growing up my mom had taught me to never take decisions based on money, to not let money drive your life, your dreams but the first opportunity I had, I had chosen money over my own security. Sorry, Mom!

But right now, I had no choice, I had to give up on my dreams and I would give up my pride if I had to, to ensure Ana didn't give up on her dreams. I would do anything, even endure a stalker quietly if that meant Ana would be able to pursue her post-graduation and settle better in life. I had no right to put my safety over her life, her career. My life was not just mine!

My heart was in dilemma and I couldn't do anything about it. I had to do this, hopefully last sacrifice for my sister and make sure she stood on her own feet. I could never show my helplessness or dilemma or else she would drop all her dreams and start working as soon as her graduation was over. I couldn't risk that. It was time to chin up and face the music. I told my heart that I could do it.

Moreover, this stalker was Yuvraj's brother, he couldn't be all that bad, right? Yuvraj was a sweetheart. How worse could his brother be? I would surely be able to navigate past him, and hopefully, his obsession with me would fizz out in a few days when he would realize how boring and uninterested, I was.

I reached the pharmacy store and found Ana and Yuvi both sitting there chatting away like no one's business. I had sought permission from the owner to let these two be at the store, while I finished my interview. He understood my need for a better-paying job this was always a temporary solution and he was happy to let me take time off and allow these two monkeys to sit for a while.

"Hey guys, how is it going?" I asked and Ana jumped out of the stool she was perched on. My little sister was tiny, barely 5 feet 1 inch tall, as opposed to my 5 feet 7 inches.

"We should be asking you that? How did the interview go?"

"I got the job!" I did a little dance.

"What? Straight job, no round two interview?" Yuvraj stood up surprised.

"I had three rounds of interviews and the final round was taken by your brother, Viraj is his name, right?"

"Yes, he interviewed you? He never does that!"

"Oh!"

"And what did he say?"

"He interviewed, he saw my designs, asked about other jobs and offered me the job!"

"Yay!" Ana came running over to hug me and Yuvi put his hands around both of us and engulfed us in a big bear hug.

"When do you have to join?" He asked when we broke our group hug.

"Next Friday!"

"Oh wow! So, one week to wrap everything else up!"

"Yes! I hope this works out."

"I haven't worked in our company, Trish, but I can promise that most people who join don't leave but ultimately retire from there, it's that kind of company and they take good care of their employees."

I smiled at his words; it might be that kind of company but he had no inkling that his brother whom he adored so much was my stalker. And I didn't have the heart to burst his bubble. I had to wait and watch how working in the same company went. I had asked him today to stop stalking me and he had replied that he would try, as if I was asking him to give up everything he held dear.

The week went by quickly as I spoke to the college administration team and submitted my resignation. They were all aware of my condition and that I was actively seeking a full-time job and this was just a pitstop for me, though they were upset to let me go and having to find someone so quickly they were also happy that I had got an offer from such a prestigious company and I could pursue my dreams. Some of the admin staff members mentioned that Viraj Rajvansh had made a personal donation a couple of months back to the college, to fund repair of the old building.

I had studied in this college and I was the college topper, they all knew me for a long time and had seen my struggle from an early age, when I was in my final year and my mom had expired, leaving me in no state to continue college or further studies. I had joined a part-time job back then too and appeared for the exams alongside it. Still, it was a pleasant surprise for everyone when I had managed to emerge topper of the college. The faculty had always been very supportive and encouraging.

Deeksha Di came home to meet me the day before I had joined work and she brought along some of her Indian wear suits. She was almost built the same as me, slim, and tall. She was married and mostly only wore Indian wear at her place. She had several good suits that she barely ever used and thought now that I had to go to the office every day, I could use them once in a while.

Ana and I had gone shopping a day earlier and bought some formal Western clothes for the office, so now with these traditional outfits also added in the mix, my small wardrobe was overflowing, and so was my heart with the love of all my near and dear ones. How blessed was I that everyone was overjoyed with my achievement?

My dad was the only one unaffected by all of this as the first thing he had asked when I said I got the job was if they will pay me more. Ana had shaken her head in negative and I knew better than to tell him how much more I would earn. So, I blatantly lied –

"No Baba, money is very low, but the job will have security and I will learn better."

"What will you do with learning better? Do two or three odd jobs to earn better!"

"Okay Baba, I will work here for a few months and then change again."

"Yes, look for a job that pays more, I need more money, I am in debt already!"

"Okay, Baba!"

I wasn't proud of my lying but I had to. If I had told him I earned better, all the extra money that I planned on saving to pay off the education loan and for Ana's higher studies would go down the drain in the purchase of liquor and I was not ready to take that risk. No, he won't be able to ever find out how much I get paid and this was for the best.

It was the last day I was at the pharmacy before I joined work and I was practicing a sketch when I heard a throat clear. I stiffened, thinking the stalker had walked up and looked up only for relief to wash over me. Alok stood there smiling at me.

"Hey!" I looked around, he never came to the pharmacy or met me in open because he feared that someone from his office or dad's acquaintance would see him with me and spill the beans to his dad before he had mentioned himself.

"I came to wish you good luck!" He slid across a gift wrapped in golden paper.

"Alok, I don't need this."

"Keep it, I will be happy. You need all the good luck, you are going to work for Viraj Rajvansh, I have heard he is a tyrant and works people to their bones. Be careful, one mistake and he throws people out too." I gulped as nervousness took hold inside me. Viraj Rajvansh already made me nervous and now this. Alok rarely talked ill about anyone, so if he mentioned this, it must be true.

"Okay!"

"I didn't mean to scare you babes, I only meant to warn you, so you be careful. Do you need anything, I mean formal clothes or such, I can take you shopping over the weekend or I can get some clothes, you can try them at my place."

"No!" I said feeling horrified that he thought he needed to buy me clothes so I would be presentable at work. "I am sorted, I bought a few the day before."

"Proper good brands, right?"

That comment pinched and I stayed quiet, just nodding in response. His good brands meant a lakh for a shirt, he knew I could never afford it and usually, he remained cautious of what he said to me.

"I only meant in a good way, babes, these small things matter. You need to make a good impression and I always want the best for you!"

"I know, I got good formal clothes, and depending on how people dress there, I may buy some more after I get my first salary."

"Yeah, or just text me and I could quickly arrange for something. We are meeting this weekend, right?"

"Are we?" I smiled.

"Yes, I am taking you home."

Home for him meant his bachelor pad not where he lived with his parents in his extended joint family. He had taken me to his apartment a few months back after he got it furnished and we spent all day chilling out and having fun. He loved to cook, so we both tried cooking our lunch together and it was good fun. He was a good listener and always heard all my rants, providing my guidance, at times just a shoulder to lean on.

Initially, a few times were fun, when we lazed around and watched movies at his apartment but then his advances increased and his way of saying taking you home, started to mean taking you to bed. I had tried to stall his advances for a very long time but being together for almost four years and being so in love, I had given in to his advances and let him move to third and home base gradually.

I got ready for the first day of my work and hugged Ana tight, I needed the assurance that all would work out well. Just as I was about to step out, my dad looked up.

"Where did you buy new clothes from?"

I stilled. If he knew Ana and I had gone on a shopping spree he would freak out and start hitting us right away.

"Deeksha Di gave me some as a gift for the new workplace."

"Oh, do you think she has money these days?"

"Baba! No, we can't ask her for money, she only gifted because Jiju allowed her to."

Ana and I looked at each other worriedly. She nodded and gestured for me to go on.

I stepped into the magnificent Rajvansh Towers feeling slightly nervous but trying to look stylish and confident. I wore a dark blue pant suit with a light blue shirt, when in doubt go with the classics. This was my best professional look, with my hair neatly tied behind in a ponytail, small heels, and a small new bag to carry all my essentials. I didn't know if people here at work wore skirts and dresses or more of traditional dresses.

I introduced myself at the reception and I was asked to take the elevator and go to the 18th floor of the tower. I reached there and realized my desk was setup right outside CEO's cabin opposite his secretary's desk. The secretary, Rajni, was a middle-aged lady, she beamed at me and started telling me some things to keep in mind when interacting with Viraj. He was impatient, a perfectionist, and didn't like people who were lazy or slacked in their work. He was also very particular about timings and when he said he wanted something by 4, it only meant 3:59 not even 4:01. I nodded listening to it all, until the HR lady, Jyoti, I had met the other day came over with a bunch of papers for me to fill up and sign.

I got busy with it all and didn't even realize how long it had been, till Rajni, came over to my desk.

"Take a break, come I will show you where coffee machine is."

I smiled at her; I was almost done. So, I gathered all the papers and asked her if she could show me where the HR head sat at and she mentioned this floor was the executive floor and HR team sat on the other side.

What was I doing on the executive floor?

Rajni showed me Jyoti's desk from a distance, it was empty so she took me to the pantry which was a floor below ours. A nice huge pantry with bright orange and green chairs and tables set out for people to sit, relax, and have coffee. I loved the airy and open vibe this office had. I took a cup of coffee for myself and turned around to go back to my desk when my gaze fell on Jyoti, who was entering the pantry.

Rajni smiled and left.

"I came to your desk to give the documents."

"Okay, I was in a meeting. Let me take these here."

She took the documents, scanned through them, and smiled at me.

"Thanks, this is all good, by end of the day today, you will get your ID card and access to all the floors you would need. Anything else, anytime let me know."

"Thank you!"

"Do you know Viraj from before?"

I stilled and shook my head.

"No, why?"

"Just asked, he was very impressed with your designs."

I nodded. Did she mean to say I got the job because she suspected he knew me from before? Would his stalkerish ways land me in trouble here at work?

I froze as I approached my desk. He stood at my desk looking magnificent in his black suit. His back was toward me, as he looked down at my purse kept on the desk. Slowly, he raised his hand and touched the bag reverentially and I gulped, nervousness flooding me. I took a tentative step toward him and he turned around to raise his dazed eyes at me. Our gaze met and the world faded away. Something flitted through his eyes and he straightened.

"Hello, Ms. Trisha!"

"Good morning, Sir."

"You were not at your desk?" His voice stern and cold. Was I supposed to seek his permission before moving around?

"I went to give my joining papers to Jyoti and then took a cup of coffee." I mumbled unsure if this would be counted as me making an excuse.

"In my cabin!"

I kept the coffee cup on my desk and started walking behind him, only for him to pause and turn.

"Get your coffee, it'll go cold."

I had lost all my urge to have that damn coffee.

"I don't want it now." I gritted and walked behind him, only to find Rajni in his cabin at his desk arranging something. I stilled at the door, as he spoke to Rajni sweetly and she turned to look at me.

"She came in early and has finished all the joining formalities." She spoke softly to Viraj and he nodded.

"I heard!"

Rajni left the cabin leaving me alone with him and I shifted nervously at the door.

He gestured towards a wooden partition in the room on the left side and I followed him.

A huge worktable sat there with two comfortable chairs.

"This is my designing desk, I got another chair for you, this is where we will work from."

I gulped; we will work together. From his cabin? Damn!

"I have an hour now, before I have to head to a meeting, I will brief you and leave you to do some initial sketches. We can then review them in the evening."

I nodded.

"You can stay back late, right? I mean reaching home at 9, will work from here too, right?"

Reaching home at 9, every day? He expected me to work 12 hours a day. I knew he was referring to my work hours from the pharmacy shop perspective and I had no response for him.

"Won't work?" He raised an eyebrow when he didn't get any response from me.

"It will work!" I gulped, nervousness flooding my veins.

"Good, because I like to design in the evenings!"

He gestured for me to sit and removed his coat, hung it on the back of his chair and got down to folding his shirt sleeves. I looked at his corded muscled forearms as inch by inch his fair skin sprinkled with generous hair was revealed to my gaze from under his light blue shirt.

He chuckled and I looked up at him, to find his gaze on me. Shoot! He was smiling because he thought I was interested in him too. I needed to be careful, I thought as I turned my gaze away from him.

He got down to explaining to me his vision for the new line he wanted to launch. Rajvansh textiles had ventured into the ready-made garment business only about a year or two back and they launched newer designs as per the season. They had hired a team of designers, but everything went through Viraj himself because he was too finicky about the designs, quality, material, and such.

"Nothing but the best for our customers!"

I nodded understanding that emotion well.

After explaining his thought process, he showed me some sketches and said –

"I want you to design something on these lines, something bold, something for those who want to make a statement with their fashion choices! Not for the common public, but for those who want to stand out in a crowd."

I nodded as he rolled down his sleeves, put on his coat, and walked out of his cabin for whatever meeting he had to go to.

I didn't see him all day, as Rajni told me he returned briefly to his cabin when I had gone to the cafeteria to get my lunch. The cafeteria was huge and on multiple floors providing various cuisines of food, live counters, and healthy food options all at subsidized rates for the employees. I tried a Mexican burrito bowl today, which was amazing and I was determined to explore more food options here.

In the evening at around 6, when he had not returned, I got up to leave. Stacking all my sketches and putting them inside a folder. I decided to leave the folder on the desk in case he came back and wanted to look. I tidied up the desk and just as I was about to open his cabin door, it burst open and there he stood. The door hit me on my forehead and I stumbled back.

"I am so sorry! Are you hurt?" He was next to me that very second.

I shook my head and stepped back but he caught hold of my hands and removed them from my forehead to survey the damage. Then shocking the daylights out of me, he pressed his big palm on my forehead and cradled my head in his other arm. He stood so close to me that I could feel the heat of his body seeping through the layer of my clothes. I tried to step back; he didn't even realize how close he stood as his focus was on my head.

"Better?"

I nodded. His proximity was making me nervous. I didn't want him in my space, touching me.

"I am okay!" I stepped several steps back and he had to let go of my face. His gaze then roamed over every inch of my body slowly making me far more nervous than before.

"I... I made three sketches!" I blurted to just get his focus to shift away from my body. His shameless pursuit made me want to hide. I was fully clothed and covered but his pursual was making me feel hot and bothered.

"Show me!"

I walked up to the work desk and opened the folder for him. He laid out all three sketches on the desk, side by side and studied them closely, his face showing no expression at all.

Then he turned his face to me and I saw annoyance all over it.

"I said I want bold designs, not these conservative ones!" His tone sharp.

I gulped. I had gone bold with the sleeves, the length of the skirts, the cut as such, what more he wanted, I looked down at the designs frowning.

He picked up a pencil and another sheet of paper and started sketching quickly like a maniac and that somehow made me want to run away from this room. He was angry and impulsively I dreaded the moment he would take that anger out on me. I was probably alone with him on this floor, now that it was so late in the evening and never had I ever felt so scared and lonely in my life.

"This... not this... do you understand?" He raised his voice and I stepped back, only for him to yank me back to him, holding both my arms.

"Don't you walk away when I am talking to you!"

"Sorry!" I blurted. I was petrified of the stronghold he had on my arms and the blaze in his eyes. I held my breath because if I left my breath, my breasts would brush up against his chest, he was holding me in a tight grip so close to him.

"I see the problem!" He brought his right hand up and dabbed his finger hard on my chest where the shirt's first button was, then his finger touched my exposed skin just above making me shiver in panic. What the heck was he doing?

Would he assault me? I knew he stalked me but I didn't think he would rape me, was he, not a big shot, a famous business tycoon, I was quacking within with fear and anxiety but I stood my ground, I would punch him in the face and knee his balls if he tried anything else. I would not let him harm me; I was determined.

"That was conservative now this is bold and stylish. Deeper necklines, shorter hems, bold cuts, and patterns, everything together makes it bold, not just making a dress sleeveless will make it bold." He ranted; anger and frustration dripping from his voice, his finger pointing to the sketches but his gaze focused on the skin under my neck. He looked up and his expression changed from furious to confusion and then of gentle care.

"What's wrong?"

I was terrified and couldn't get a word out. I just kept pulling my head back until his finger grazed my cheek and I realized a tear had slipped out.

"Are you scared?" He cupped my face. "I won't hurt you! Never!"

But I was terrified beyond comprehension. His soothing words made no difference and I kept shaking in terror unable to move away or utter a word. I just wanted to get out of here, away from him.

"Trisha!" He spoke, his voice gentle and he slowly grazed his thumb over my cheeks only to make me shake violently.

"Please!" I whimpered. I was ready to faint but I had to stay strong, if I fainted on him, he was sure to violate me.

"Am I hurting you? Scaring you?"

I managed to nod slowly. He immediately took his hands away and stepped back.

"I would never!" He took out his handkerchief and extended it to me. "I would never ever hurt you, Trisha!"

I quickly wiped my tears from the back of my hand and stepped back clutching onto my shirt.

"You want to leave for today?" He asked softly.

I nodded and he stepped away leaving space for me to walk out and I ran out of his cabin still shaking with what had just happened. He said he wouldn't hurt me, but then what the hell was that shouting like a maniac, coming onto me like an animal? He was just moment away from opening my shirt, what was he going to do? He had been stalking me for weeks now, I should not have agreed to work for him. He was some psychopath, I needed to tell Yuvi to get his brother admitted in an asylum.

I quickly gathered my things from the desk and rushed out. I was shaking with terror so bad that I had to sit in the basement for a few minutes to compose myself before being able to drive out. I needed to rethink whether to continue working for him or not.

# CHAPTER SIX

# TOUGH DECISIONS

## *Trisha*

I could barely sleep all night on Friday, I was debating whether to go back to his office on Monday or not. But one look around the house and at the sleeping form of Ana, I knew I didn't even have the choice. How could I quit and run away at the first encounter with the real world? I had grown up in a sheltered home and I was lucky that even outside, in college, in my first job, I got supportive people to offer me guidance. This was the first time; someone had been so rough and I was contemplating quitting.

I paused, what would I say to everyone, why I quit the job, no one would believe that the Rajvansh CEO would stalk me or touch me like that. I couldn't say that to my family, I couldn't jeopardize Ana's education and future. I couldn't just quit. Giving up was not option when others depended on you, giving up was never an option! I needed to be strong. He had said he wouldn't hurt me, so maybe this was it. If I stayed careful and worked around his temper then maybe I wouldn't see his beastly side often.

I needed this job, and my desperation would urge me to face him every day and be strong. I had to do this! Decision made I fell into deep sleep towards morning.

It was Saturday and after preparing lunch for Ana and my dad, I sneaked out to meet Alok, he had been pestering me to come over to his flat. I wanted to spend time with him but at his flat all he wanted was to have sex and that was painful, I didn't enjoy it. I had denied him that for very long because I was conservative, like how Viraj had accused me yesterday. I wanted to wait for marriage, that was the kind of upbringing I had had. But Alok was not ready to wait, two years into our relationship he had started demanding more, and I pushed and stalled it for more than a year after it as well.

But then, one day he almost forced himself on me. Yeah, my first time was almost a rape from my boyfriend. I had asked him to go slow, to be gentle because I was inexperienced and he kept saying he was being slow but the pain that had engulfed me had left me with a bitter taste. Maybe it wasn't for everyone. Maybe sex was just hyped up, because there was absolutely no pleasure in it, only pain. And now I dreaded it.

It always made me feel miserable after we were done and I resigned to my fate. Seeing the stars or feeling the rush of feelings was all bookish talk and nothing of the sort happened in real life. I had once confided in Deeksha di when she had seen some bruises on my neck and guessed. She knew about Alok. She was at first surprised but then when I narrated all about it, she nodded and told me that yes it was painful and she had not seen any stars in all these years of her married life either. We had made fun of it and laughed together.

Ana obviously had no clue about it, but Deeksha Di and I then often shared our experiences and our problems and we were convinced that to see those stars we needed to continue reading the romance novels and go to bed for the fizzle and pain.

As I knocked on Alok's door, I heard him talking on the phone on the other side, or was someone home? If someone was home, then probably I needed to walk right back and somehow, I felt relieved to do that. But I saw when he opened the door, he was alone and, on the phone, he gestured me in, raising a finger to his lips to ask me to stay quiet. I nodded and proceeded to plop myself on the black couch he had in his living room.

There was a big box of pizza and some cold drink bottles already there. Was he waiting for me or someone else? He joined me on the couch and pulled me into his lap as he kissed me, his hands sliding inside my t-shirt on the back.

"Who else is coming?" I asked when we came up for air.

"No one, why?"

"Pizza?"

"For you and me! I plan on working up our appetite!" He grinned and I lost my heart out to him yet again. He had a boyish charm which he seldom showed. He stood up suddenly and I looked up at him, he was tall almost 6 feet 3 inches tall, and muscular. He picked me up as if I weighed nothing.

"What are you doing!" I laughed.

"Taking you where I want you the most!"

He laid me down on the bed in his bedroom and proceeded to remove his clothes first before getting down to removing mine.

"Can we please?"

"What babes?"

"I am not in the mood, now."

"Periods?"

"No, no!"

"Then I will get you in the mood." He didn't listen until he had me, like he wanted, naked and spread out for him. He sheathed his length with protection.

He kissed me hard as his body pressed into mine. He trailed his tongue down my jaw and my neck as sensations erupted deep in my core, I loved this foreplay. I clutched his shoulder and pushed my head back. I wanted more of these soft nuzzles and kisses. But the next moment I felt searing pain as he pushed his length in my core. I jumped slightly on the bed and he pushed me back down, taking my beaded nip in his mouth.

"You feel so good!" He mumbled and started moving within me.

I adjusted myself, trying to relax my body to stop the pain. I knew if I didn't clutch my muscles so hard, I would feel less pain, I just needed to relax. He increased his tempo and my mind went blank. I moaned as he bit my nipple and blew air on it.

He grunted with a final stroke and collapsed on me with a roar. He emptied himself within me, well within the protection that he wore but whatever. I stayed still under his weight, feeling conflicted. I was glad this was over with and yet I felt restless as I didn't find any release, any calm that he was feeling right now.

For a moment I had wanted to empty my mind too, I was not enjoying anything today because I had so much on my mind, and I chastised myself that I was thinking about another man when I was in bed with my boyfriend.

"Oh, babe, I love you so much!" Alok nuzzled his head in my neck and I melted at the warmth in his voice.

He was the only one who treated me like I was precious like I was special, so what if he didn't satisfy me sexually? He pampered me otherwise and treated me well.

We cleaned up and he sat me in his lap as I narrated my first day leaving out the scary bits of Viraj to him and ate pizza. He knew I loved pizza, and being from the background that I came from and the struggle I was currently in, he knew I never ate pizza on my own.

"I don't know Viraj closely, our families know each other, just because of the businessmen circle, you know!"

I nodded.

"But I have heard from a lot of people that he is quite a taskmaster, he pushes people to work hard, he himself works some 14 to 18 hours a day at a minimum and his world revolves around just a handful of people. He is famous for his Casanova lifestyle but no commitment guy!"

I hummed non-committedly resting my head on his shoulder. He stroked my back softly and then slid his fingers inside the t-shirt again drawing patterns on my bare skin.

"They have a huge cafeteria, spread on two floors with lots of cuisine options."

"That's nice! Yes, they are big, in a different league altogether. Is it at a subsidized rate?"

"Yes, very minimal."

"Nice, then try out all the cuisines, it would be a good change for you!"

"Then I will put on weight!"

"It will look good on you; I will have more to hold and more to love!"

I hid my face in his neck as he kissed my forehead.

We sat there chatting and dreaming about our future together. He needed another six months to settle into his business, that he had joined with his dad before broaching the topic of our marriage. He asked me to keep patience and to wait and I was willing to do that. I was in no hurry of marriage myself; I had just started my career too. Six months also sounded good to me, by then I would have settled down in Rajvansh Textiles or at least would know for sure if I needed to look for a change. I would surely have learned something by then to be able to move on to another job.

Once, Ana was in her master's and the education loan was paid off, I could breathe a little easy and focus on my life. Till then, I was happy with the arrangement we currently had. At least he was here for me, a big support emotionally.

Deeksha Di knocked on the door and stood there smiling. I was home alone today, it was a Sunday and Ana had gone to Ritika's house to finish some project, while dad was wherever he was. Dad rarely stayed home anytime and we were all in a way glad about it.

"How are you?"

She grinned as she took out a hot case.

"What did you bring?"

"Lunch for all three of us. Where is Ana?"

"She is at Ritika's house, working on a project."

"Will she come home for lunch?"

"Now, she will." I smiled as I sent a message to Ana that Deeksha Di was here.

I made some tea and both of us settled on our small couch in the living room to talk about our lives, we shared everything and spoke often. But talking face to face with your sister felt more real and connected.

She touched her cold finger on a bruise, that I didn't know I had on my upper arm.

"Alok?"

I nodded.

"Is he good? What is he saying about marriage."

"We spoke about it yesterday, he says he needs about six months to settle down at work and then will talk to his parents, that works well for me too. By then, I would have cleared Ana's loan."

"I wish I could help!"

"No, not needed. You know we wouldn't feel comfortable taking Jiju's money. It's okay, once the loan is done and if I stay in this job, soon, we would have saved up good amount."

"If you stayed in this job?" Panic flitted in her eyes.

"I mean if they don't kick me out!" I laughed to make light of her worries.

"Trisha? What is it?"

"The CEO is scary."

"Scary?"

"He scolded me so bad because my design was not bold enough, he seems like a taskmaster."

"Hard work never scared you, Trish. Is there something else?"

All my loved ones shortened my name and called me Trish, I loved it though I didn't understand how much shorter it became by just dropping an "a".

"No, Di, what will it be, it's just been a day."

"Trish, promise me, you will tell me if there is anything. If he is bad to you, you don't have to endure, just leave, and we will do something else. I will ask Raj for help!"

I nodded as I smiled, wondering if touching me and grabbing me the way he had counted as him being bad or not. I gulped, I couldn't tell di anything, though I wanted to confide and get this off my chest, but she would worry. She would panic if she knew he made me cry on the very first day of my job.

I never cried; I was the strongest of the three sisters. Ana was naïve, impulsively, sheltered, and fun-loving, while di was the softest one of the hearts. Di was the quiet, enduring type but not as strong as I was when it came to facing the world.

"Raj and I are trying for a baby!" She suddenly blurted and I grinned.

"Wow! So, lots of..." I laughed and she blushed.

"Not, lot but yeah...my mother-in-law is eating my head but won't give us any peace or a moment alone either." She cribbed and I laughed.

Her mother-in-law was like the typical one you saw in Hindi movies, always keeping her on her toes, sweet talking in front of relatives and friends but extremely rude and rigid when alone. But at least she didn't torture her physically, only verbal taunts and making her do all the household chores. Jiju loved her and pampered her well, she had lucked out with her arranged marriage and I was so happy that she had a stable life and was well settled.

Di would be a wonderful mother; she always was of a caring and nurturing nature. Even when mom was around, she had been like a second mom to me and Ana. She pampered us all and cooked delicious food, which we craved even now. I had learned cooking because mom passed away suddenly and though I could cook well enough and a good variety of Indian food, Deeksha Di had magic in her hands. Using the same ingredients, she would make the curry or dal taste much better than any of us.

Ana was our pampered princess, who could barely cook a proper meal. Shortcuts, she was very good at, helping us in the kitchen she was good at. Like she always said, all great chefs needed a helper and she was that. We just hoped she married into a family where her help and assistance could make her survive.

"Di!" Ana entered the house and rushed over to hug Deeksha Di.

She quickly freshened up as I warmed up the food and served it on three plates. All of us just settled on the floor and ate the food to our heart's content.

"Di you have magic in your hands!" Ana said the words out loud that I was thinking. "I mean Trish also cooks amazing, but this is next level amazing, right Trish!"

"I cook decently, not amazing. And yes, this is divine, a simple *paneer bhurji, dal makhani* and *roti*, bliss!" I closed my eyes as I relished the taste one last time before getting up to clear the plates.

"I will try to bring food more often!"

"No, no. That's not what we meant." Ana quickly said.

"You just come to see us more often and we are happy!" I added nodding at Ana.

We would never want her to bring us food and get in trouble herself. Her mother-in-law cared for us sisters but we didn't want her to make a fuss about Deeksha Di cooking and giving us food, often.

We sat huddled together chatting and didn't even realize it was starting to get dark outside, when Jiju knocked on our door.

"Jiju!" Ana flung herself on him and he caught her, swirling her around like a kid. He laughed as he came inside.

"Are you all done talking or do you need more time?"

"We didn't even realize the time." Di quickly got up to stand.

"Jiju, sit, I will make tea."

"No, I have booked evening show tickets, I want my wife back now."

"How romantic!" Ana sighed and I laughed while Di blushed hiding her gaze from us.

Rajveer Jiju was a cute, quiet loving type who would rarely show his love and concern. But he did these small things for Di often, because he knew it wasn't easy for her to be cooped up with his mom all day long.

Di and Jiju waved us bye as they got into their blue Wagon-R car and Ana and I stood smiling.

"I am so happy for her!" I sighed.

"Yes, I just want someone as good as Raj Jiju!" Ana acknowledged and I thought if Alok would be like this after marriage or not.

# CHAPTER SEVEN

# Bringing Her Defences Down

## *Viraj*

She stood combing her long tresses in front of the mirror dressed in a short red dress. I came to a stop behind her and her gaze met mine, as colour rose in her cheeks. I wound my hands around her waist as I pulled her close to my aroused body and she melted against me, surrendering completely.

My hands touched her peaked nips and she moaned; I moved my hands up to pull her dress down from her right shoulder. I kissed her exposed skin, ahh, it tasted delicious. Her scent was enticing wanting me to bury myself deep inside her, I bit hard on her shoulder and she gasped my name. I wanted to make her scream my name in ecstasy over and over again. I was so obsessed with her that I was going to mark every inch of her body, claim her, and make her mine.

I picked her up and laid her on the bed, burying my face in the nook of her shoulder, and taking a deep whiff of her luscious hair. She moaned at this simple act and my hands trailed down the slight curve of her hip. I wanted to touch all of her, kiss each and every inch, love it, and worship it. I moved my hands up her bare thighs, I wanted her so bad.

"Oh Viraj, I want you!"

"I want you too, Trisha!" I crashed my lips on her.

But she melted away and my lips crashed on my pillow. I woke up with a start, my body hard and sweating with desire. I looked around, of course, she was nowhere there, and the way I had behaved with her, I had a long way to go before I could have her here in my room, in my bed.

Damn it! I had totally lost my cool on Friday.

It was Monday morning and I reached the office early by 7 AM to be able to get a glimpse of her as she came. I hoped she would come in. I had spent the entire weekend in a restless state as her terrified eyes haunted me all the time. I had crossed a line; I had no right to touch her or grab her arms like that to make her shake in fear.

She came from a middle-class background and obviously, she was not like one of those I was used to meeting in the clubs, who would be happy if I touched them and spread their legs if I undid even one button. I was wrong, even though my intentions were not. I saw sheer talent in her designs but that day when she had drawn those sketches, I could see her holding back, she was too focused on making them look pretty and was not letting her real talent show.

I asked for bold designs and she for some reason had not thought through before sketching those, I knew she was capable of far better designs and I had lashed out at her, a big mistake because the next thing I saw was tears in her beautiful eyes. The eyes that I wanted to see smiling had tears because of me. I never wanted to see those grey eyes glistening with tears of fear and pain and I caused them, I felt helpless as I wiped her tears, I didn't know what to do with her, how to tell her how much I cared, how I obsessed over her.

I wanted to apologize properly and convince her that I would never do any of those things that were terrifying her, I wanted to hold her close and wipe her tears but she was shaking with fear and I knew I had lost her at that moment. Nothing I said then would have made sense to her, so I let her go. I wanted to go with her and drop her home, but she was not in a state to remain anywhere close to me and I had stepped back. I saw her walk out of my cabin feeling utterly shattered. I had found her after so long, and the first day I had hurt her, made her cry. This had to change, my ways had to change!

I just hoped that the weekend would have made her relax and she would give me a chance to apologize to her. I saw her walk in at around 8:45, dressed in a beautiful white embroidered Indian traditional long suit with stylish pants. Her big silver *Jhumkas* caressed her cheeks every time she took a step. Just a tinge of pink lipstick and kohl in her eyes was all the makeup she had and she looked enchanting and bewitching. She was so pure, so beautiful that she needed no makeup to enhance her beauty. Her long hair was open at her back and I wanted to run my fingers through her tresses, but that had to wait.

I was watching her from my desk, my cabin had a window, next to the door, that opened towards the floor, and I had always kept the blinds closed but not today. Today, I had them slightly open, such that I had a clear view of outside but from outside people would really need to peep in to see my cabin or my desk.

I waited for her to settle down and wanted to watch her to my heart's content. She wore flat shoes, but still, she was tall and slim. She walked in confidently just looking at my closed door once. She turned on the computer at her desk and folded her hands, stealing a piece of my heart at her simple gesture. She had not realized that I was watching her through the partially open blinds. I filled my heart and mind with images of her, when she was relaxed and calm, not shaking with fear because of me.

I walked out of my cabin and she jumped up from her desk.

"Good morning, Trisha! How are you?" I spoke softly.

"Good morning, Sir!"

"Viraj, call me, Viraj. You want to join me for coffee?"

"No, thanks. I just came."

"That's okay, come have coffee then we can work."

She looked at the empty floor nervously.

"Trisha, look, I am sorry for Friday, I didn't mean to scare you or hurt you. I never will. I just felt you were holding back and not expressing yourself properly in those designs."

"It's okay!" She said automatically, her voice small and soft.

"It's not okay to yell or scare you, let me make it up, come join me for coffee?"

She nodded her head and walked around her desk to join me.

"Did you eat your breakfast?"

"I ate at home." She replied.

"Who all do you have at home?"

"My dad and my younger sister!"

"Nice! I have a younger brother."

"I know."

"You do?"

"Yeah, he is in the same college I studied in and was recently working there in the library."

"Ahh, right!" And the visual from six months back of her dancing in the basement room came into my mind. She had worn a similar Indian suit back then as well.

"I will make!" She said stepping close to the coffee machine as I picked up two mugs. I passed her the mug and our fingers brushed slightly. "Sugar?"

"Yeah, half spoon, thanks!" I mumbled watching her unashamedly while she prepared a cup of coffee for me. What would I not do to see this every day?

"Here!" She said and quickly kept the cup on the table in front of me, not allowing me to take it from her hand. She was on the defensive.

We stepped out talking about her education and work experience after taking our coffee and when we approached my cabin, I noticed Rajni was in already.

"Good morning, Viraj, you came in early?"

"Good morning, yes, I needed a file; I had left here!" It was a white lie, but who cared?

"And you have taken your coffee."

"I needed it badly didn't want to wait up for you. How does my day look like today?"

I noticed Trisha slowly slipping behind her desk quietly sipping her coffee. She closed her eyes smiling softly relishing the taste, as the coffee hit her buds and I memorized that she liked coffee with milk and one heaped spoon of sugar.

It had been three weeks since she was working here and I had gone very easy on her after the first day's debacle. She was opening up to me and working hard. I had offered her a drop back home, but she insisted on going back on her *Activa*, I sometimes followed her still, to ensure she reached home fine.

She didn't talk much with me, but I noticed her talking to Rajni, Jyoti and a few other ladies on the floor. She was always humble and polite, no matter how much I pushed her to work harder and her designs were truly amazing, I loved each one of them though I pushed her to do better.

It was a Friday today and as I walked into the cafeteria, my gaze fell on her, she sat in a corner with Rajni eating her lunch. She wore a short lime-yellow top with blue jeans. It was the first time I was seeing her in jeans at work today and it suited her well. Everything suited her so well, that I was sure I would find her attractive, even if she wrapped a garbage bag and stepped out one fine day. I was so smitten, that I spent hours at the end watching her either work on the design table inside my cabin or when I was on calls, she would sit out at her desk but my gaze would always be focused on her.

I slid next to her on the bench and she stiffened.

"Hi ladies, I hope I can join you both!"

She just looked at me, shocked while Rajni laughed happily.

"Of course! How come you are eating here today?"

"I just wanted to walk around a bit, too many calls since morning." I had rushed through my last call when I had seen her and Rajni walking out for lunch. I knew they ate in the cafeteria every day, and I had this urge to join her, to eat with her, to see what she liked to eat.

"Why aren't you eating?" I asked her when I noticed she had suddenly stopped eating and was looking at her phone.

She looked up trying to focus back on me.

"Oh, sorry!" She kept her phone aside and quietly started to eat.

"What's the matter?"

"My result came, was checking the marks."

"And?"

"They are good, so good!"

"Congratulations!" I put my hand forward and she looked at her own hand checking if it was dirty or not.

"Thanks!"

"Congratulations Trisha, this calls for a treat!" Rajni gushed and she nodded back at her, smiling.

She had not smiled at me!

I was in a meeting with our Marketing Head and as he left, my gaze sought her outside only to freeze.

Yuvraj sat perched on her desk and held her hand. Rage coursed through my body and I stepped closer to the partially opened blinds to check what was going on. He held her hand and was tying something on it, while she sat there laughing and looking at him with pure unadulterated adoration. What the heck!

She never smiled at me, and here she was laughing at whatever my brother was saying! He was a charmer but he was younger than her. She only looked at me terrified, not once tenderly, even when I was good to her.

Jealousy reared its head and I burned within, wanting to ask them to step away and wanting to thrash my brother for touching my girl, for making my girl laugh when I had not even earned one smile from her. I was jealous of my own brother!

I paused. My girl? Was she, my girl? Not yet, but I was determined to make her mine. No one else could have her when I had been pining for her since close to eight months now. I watched them both but they were lost in their world and she kept laughing at his antics and I couldn't take it anymore. I opened the door of my cabin and they both looked up at me.

"What's going on here?"

"Bhai!" Yuvraj jumped off her desk and stood grinning at me.

"Why didn't you come inside, Yuvi?" I asked in as normal tone as I could muster.

"Oh, I know better than to disturb you when you are working Bhai, I only came to meet her today."

I glared at her and she stood up nervously behind my brother. Her left-hand clutching something on her right wrist. Ahh, there was a new shiny bracelet there, probably what he was making her wear!

"I guess it's time for you to get back to work!" Yuvi smiled at her, oblivious to the tension in the room. She looked at him and smiled.

"When will I see you again?" She asked in a small whisper.

"Whenever you want, your wish is my command!" He dramatically bowed in front of her, and she giggled. "Okay Bhai, I will get going, and you can have her back! Just don't make her work too much!" He smiled, came forward hugged me, and walked away waving her a bye.

She waved at him but pulled her hand down as her soft gaze met my raging one. I was spitting mad and walked back into my cabin to cool myself down. I couldn't talk to her or else I would trash her and worse make her cry again. I needed to calm myself down before talking to her.

I poured some whiskey into a glass and sat at my desk sipping it and controlling my urge to talk to her. Yuvraj was younger than her, and surely it didn't mean a thing. I needed her to look at me like she was looking at my brother. I needed her to smile and laugh at my words and wave me bye every time I left.

A brief knock startled me and I realized I had been drinking whiskey for almost an hour now, lost in my thoughts.

"Yes!"

"Viraj!" She stood at the door unsure whether to come in or run. Her gaze met mine then settled on the whiskey bottle at my desk and something shifted in her gaze. She took a step back. "I will come later!"

"Trisha, come, I was about to call you."

She stood nervously at the door her gaze darting between me and the bottle, panic rising in her. What was it? I stood up, picked up the bottle, locked it up in the bar cabinet at the corner, and walked towards the desk.

She came in and stood with her sketches in hand. I had a look at them but surprised her with my question.

"So, how do you know my brother exactly?"

"He... he is my sister's friend. He often comes to pick up and drop her, so we have met."

"And?"

"And now we are friends of sorts!"

"Boyfriend?"

"No!" She stumbled upon shocked. Ahh, thank God, she was genuinely surprised! "Just a friend, good friend. My sister and he are not boyfriend and girlfriend!" She added and I frowned.

I grabbed both her elbows and pulled her to me; she was not expecting it and came crashing on me. Her soft body melted my hard burning planes. I wound a hand behind her back and she struggled to get away. As I leaned down, she scrunched her nose and moved her face away from me. I was losing my control today, with her looking so deliciously beautiful.

"I asked what he was to you; not about your sister!"

"Let me go! He is just a friend!"

"Just a friend, so he came to meet you and went away without meeting his brother!" I grabbed her chin and turned her face to me.

Why was she not looking at me?

"Please let me go!" She whimpered.

I loosened my grip she quickly jumped back maintaining distance between us. I was losing control and she was scared again.

"Why was he here?" I tried hard to control my libido and calm myself down.

"He came to congratulate me for my marks, my sister must have told him and to gift me this." She raised her wrist to show a beautiful bracelet on her wrist. I grabbed her wrist without thinking and ran my thumb over it settling on the pulse point, making her jump and fidget to get her arm free of my hold.

"I didn't ask for it. He got it, I didn't know. He said it is silver, I don't know how much it would have cost him. I am sorry, I will return it back to him!"

What was she blabbering on?

"Why will you return if he is your friend?"

"Because its silver and it might be expensive. I am sorry, I don't want any favours, or money or please just let me go!" She whimpered and I dropped her wrist. She was so nervous now that her words were not clear and she looked ready to faint. She slowly removed the bracelet and kept it on the table in front of me.

Damn it!

I focused better, I was messing it all up yet again. She thought I had a problem with my brother gifting her a silly silver bracelet, she thought my problem was with spending money. She had no idea I was ready to cover every inch of her body in platinum and diamonds only if she allowed me. I looked at her closely and realized she was terrified of me right now.

"Relax, I didn't mean this. I wasn't even asking for money, or expensive. This is not expensive and I am embarrassed my brother is gifting such silly things to his friends." I picked up the bracelet and took her hand in mine to wrap it back on her wrist.

"I..." She tried to pull her hand away, but I was having none of it. Ever since I saw Yuvi tying this bracelet on her wrist, I had been dying to do the same.

"Relax, I was just curious to know why he was here and he ran away as he saw me. This is pretty, looks nice on you!" I ran a thumb over it and she fidgeted again.

"Do I scare you?"

Her eyes went big then she shook her head averting her gaze and looking down at her clasped fingers.

"No!"

"Then why are you so ready to run away?" I held her chin between my thumb and index finger to make her look at my face.

"The smell!"

"Of whiskey?"

"Of what I don't know, but you are..." She frowned, then took a deep breath, gathering all her courage as shutters fell on her eyes, "I am not scared of you!"

"Then why do you never relax and talk to me, how you were talking to him? I heard you laugh for the first time today!"

Our gaze met, surprise flicking through them. Did she not know how obsessed I was with her? Did she not know how much she affected me?

"I... you are... I mean... just you!"

"I am listening!"

"I don't know, I guess you scare me a little!" She sighed all fight leaving her body as her shoulders slumped. I didn't like this version of her, being tired and defeated.

"I don't mean to. I will never hurt or harm you. I get angry but it's just about work!" I spoke as softly as I could. I needed her to not run away, to not get scared of me. That was the last thing I wanted.

She nodded choosing silence yet again.

"Yuvraj is fun-loving and very warm-natured, he is still enjoying his life with no responsibility on his shoulders. I am not like him, I have a thousand things to take care of, even as a kid, I didn't have it as easy as he had and guess the difference shows." I continued, I didn't understand why I had this urge for her to know me, to understand me, and to validate me.

"I know, I understand what you mean!"

"You do?" My voice showed the surprise I felt.

"Yeah, I am the middle child, my elder sister is married and happy in her home, and my younger sister is in college, happy, fun-loving, chilled out how a college student should ideally be, like Yuvi. And me, I don't know what it is to be so carefree, I have responsibilities on my shoulders, I need to earn so we can eat, so we can pay our bills, so I can clear off the loan, so I can save up for..." She looked up and immediately clammed up as if she had never intended to share. "I am sorry, why am I telling you all this!"

"I know, I understand what you mean!" I smiled as I used her words and she smiled back slightly in response.

What responsibilities and loans, was she talking about? I had been going crazy not knowing a thing about her all this while, and today while she gave me a brief glimpse she clammed up as if she didn't want to share. Why?

"Your dad?"

"He doesn't work!" Her reply came out all too fast and I knew better than to prod further.

"Trisha, any time you need something, help, money, just an ear to rant, I am here."

She looked up surprised at my words then smiled.

"Thanks, hopefully, I won't need the first two and I won't bore you with the last one."

"I would love it if you did!"

She chuckled.

We sat down to work together. I tried to show her my vision for the new line of clothes I wanted to design for men. She focused well, learned quickly, and always asked a lot of questions when it came to work and designing and I liked it about her, because her questions often made me think more, ponder more and come up with better ideas.

I stepped away when my phone buzzed and she picked up the pencil to finish up the sketch I had started to do. I watched her from a few feet away, as I spoke to Naman. I again noticed she was holding herself back and sticking to conventional styles, not letting her wild side take over. I finished the call and stood behind her watching. Impulsively, I covered her right hand with mine as I held the pencil to make the strokes bolder. She stiffened in her spot.

"Longer, let it be long and creative, Trisha, why do you hold back, these are sketches, these are meant to be creative, bold, and striking, don't confine yourself to a conservative approach or practicality of it all." I ranted next to her ear as I maneuvered her hand to draw.

I turned my face to see her as she had completely stilled and possibly stopped breathing. My heart was galloping so fast that I was sure she would hear it in this stunned silence. Her face was so close to mine, lips right within my reach if I moved mine just an inch.

Her shocked gaze met mine and my heart flipped in my chest. Her beautiful grey eyes had golden specks on them that glittered up close. Her soft warm breath touched my face and filled my senses with her citrusy fragrance of green apple. A few moments passed as our gaze remained locked. I saw confusion and terror flit through her eyes until she calmed down and her eyes blankly stared at me invoking emotions, I didn't know I was capable of.

I moved my fingers slowly up her right wrist and she shuddered under my touch, her skin erupting in goosebumps. She shut her eyes and didn't bolt away, making me want to pursue this further. She was so still that if not for her goosebumps, one would think my touching her was not affecting her at all. I trailed a finger up her forearm and cupped her elbow with my hand.

"No!" She whispered and I paused. "Please don't!" She spoke and I took my hand away.

However, obsessed I was with her, I knew the word no meant no. She was asking me to stop and that was what I was going to do. I saw surprise flicker through her eyes as she saw me take my hand away and step back at her words. Did she think I wouldn't stop when she said no? Did she think I was capable of forcing her? What sort of a monster did she think I was?

She sat there frowning, gathering her courage, trying hard not to panic, and running away. Her gaze remained locked at the sketch but I knew her mind was far away, lost in her thoughts. I watched her for a few moments, as she tried to gather herself and looked up at me. Was that disappointment I just saw in her eyes? Or was that shame?

"Shall we work on this tomorrow?" I asked unsure of what was happening to me, what was going on in her mind.

"If you are okay with it?" she asked.

I nodded. I stepped away to go back to my desk and she quickly gathered up her things and tidied the desk to leave.

I felt numb and stunned at the range of emotions I felt today, as I touched her hand, they were new to me, I had never wanted someone so desperately, and it wasn't lust, it wasn't the primal desire of the body. It was more, it was beyond the words my mind could comprehend at the moment. I wanted to touch not just her skin but her heart, mind, and soul. And I know very well that she let me touch only her skin, I was not at all in her mind or heart, let alone the soul. She sat still and I was quite sure that when she shut her eyes, it was not to savour the sensations I was evoking but to block me out.

I sat there long after she had left thinking about how she had reacted. She had shuddered under my touch, she felt a tsunami of emotions just like I had as I ran a finger up her arms, for a moment there, I felt her close her eyes and surrender to my touch until something had changed and she looked guilty and conflicted.

I was falling so hard and fast for her, but I was sure she wasn't with me at that moment when she shut her eyes. She had distanced herself, blocked herself out when I touched her for some reason.

Did she have someone in her life? Maybe a boyfriend? I panicked at the thought, but yes, she had panicked too. She had liked my touch but then looked at my hand as if feeling guilty for liking something she was not supposed to like.

Damn it, no she couldn't have a boyfriend! What would that make me?

It was a Sunday afternoon, when I sat on the balcony reading a book, the breeze was good and it wasn't sunny either. Yuvraj walked up to me and asked if he could join.

"How come, you are home today?"

"The exams are approaching, so kind of busy studying, no one wanted to go out."

"Prepared for the exams?"

"Yeah, I will rock it!"

I smiled; I loved him but I rarely knew what to talk to him about.

"Bhai, that day, I came to your office to meet Trisha, you weren't angry right?"

"Why would I be angry with you coming to our office?"

"No, I mean you didn't get angry on her, right? She was working, she didn't know I would show up and she was shocked. She kept urging me to go back because it would waste her time, she should have been working."

I narrowed my eyes, why was he so worried about her? And why was she so worried about work and time? Everyone in the office wasted so much time, gossiping, moving around, and socializing anyway. Did she not do any of that? Then I remembered, I had swamped her with so much work that she wouldn't have done that ever.

"You didn't get mad at her after I left right?"

"Why do you think I would have gotten mad at her?"

"Because I saw rage in your eyes, and I saw how she had panicked when you walked out of your cabin. She is an angel, Bhai, please don't ever get mad at her, for me."

"What's going on, Yuvi? Do you like her or something?"

"No! She is like my sister, my elder sister, I love her like that. She is a pure soul, very soft-hearted though she shows the world that she is made of steel. She has had a very tough life and she is struggling but would never complain, never utter a word."

"Tell me properly, what struggles?"

Yuvraj then narrated how her mother died suddenly a few years back, while her father met with an accident the same night, and how her entire world collapsed around her in the blink of an eye. Her father was an alcoholic, who didn't work, didn't earn. She was the only one earning in the family and she had cut short her education to take a loan for her sister's education and hence had been working multiple jobs to support them all. My heart twisted in pain as Yuvraj sat painting the horrid story of her life, I had no clue about.

"Why did you never help them?"

"Ana, I manage to but Trisha is too proud to take even a penny from me. She would sell herself off before asking for money from everyone."

My breath got stuck in my throat at his words. She would sell herself off, no, I would never let that happen, I needed to make her open up to me, talk to me. That was why she had thought I was objecting to that silver bracelet that Yuvi gave her because she was having trouble accepting a big gift. A big gift from her perspective, and absolute peanuts from our perspective.

"Doesn't Trisha have anyone else, a boyfriend or someone she could depend on?" I took my chance and asked the one thing that had given me sleepless nights.

"Not that I am aware of and even if she had a boyfriend, she would hesitate to take a dime from him. I know her. Ana is fun, I take her out, feed her good food, or buy her some tops, and some dresses sometimes, and she doesn't think too much about it, but not Trisha, she insists on feeding me when I go to drop Ana home. She insists on buying me a birthday gift, a Diwali gift just like she buys for Ana and her sister."

"Then why just a silver bracelet, Yuvi, you could have gotten her something better, something more useful, right?"

"She wouldn't take it. Even the silver bracelet, she tried to return it yesterday, saying she took it because she loved my gesture but it was too expensive and I shouldn't be wasting my money on her."

"That's because of me!" I blurted.

Yuvraj frowned but said nothing.

"I asked her about it after you left, only to check why you had gifted her, and she thought I was worried that my kid brother was spending money on her and removed the bracelet to give it to me, saying she never asked for the money or jewellery."

"Shit!"

"I am sorry, I didn't know anything about their circumstances."

"I wanted to refer her to you because I had seen her designs, I had seen her struggles, but she wouldn't let me. She said she didn't want charity; she wanted a job on merit. She even asked me if I spoke to you after the first day when you interviewed her and thank God, I hadn't else she wouldn't have taken the job. She needs that job desperately Bhai, Ana was saying that she intends to pay off the education loan first and then start saving it for Ana's masters. Not even for herself!"

I realized how wrong I had been about everything and I needed to change my stance. If ever she needed anything, I needed her to come to me and not struggle alone. I knew what loneliness meant; I would never wish it upon her.

"Trisha?" I stood at the door of my cabin as she sat at her desk, typing something on the computer.

"Sir!" She stood up.

"Sir? Now we are back to Sir?"

"No, no!"

"Finish what you are doing and come over."

She saved and locked her computer to come stand next to me.

"I was cataloguing the designs you have approved. I scanned them all earlier today."

"Good! Come sit, I need help!"

I had been trying to design using graphics and needed a second opinion, usually I went with my gut feel but now I had her and I always looked for an opportunity to have her close to me, these days.

She wore a traditional Indian suit today, which was rare, she was almost always dressed in Formal trousers and shirts, never a skirt even. But today she wore a baby pink colour suit which made her look ethereal and enchanting. Her long curls were open and she wore a small Bindi on her forehead, giving her a soft enticing appearance.

I sat designing and she bent down to look closer from next to my chair and as I turned my gaze went straight to her cleavage which showed because the *Duppatta* she wore had slipped and she had not realized it yet. My body turned hard at a mere glance of her milky white skin, how I wanted to caress her softness. I was in the office, I had scared her enough last week, and I needed to pull my mind out of the gutter right now, I fisted my hands, slowly moved the chair back before I did something impulsively.

"I think we should move this logo down here and move this..." She leaned forward to extend her right hand and point at the monitor.

"Wait!" I stood up and she straightened as well.

"What? You asked how to change it!"

"Yes, you sit here, and do what you are suggesting." I pushed her down on my chair and stood next to her. She adjusted her dupatta and sat back down focussing on the graphic I had been tampering with. I moved behind the chair and adjusted myself, one glance and I was so hard, damn it! Now I needed to distract myself to calm my body back down, the periodic table, I started repeating it backwards in my head.

The door burst open after a brief knock and Rohit stood at the door shocked. I straightened but Trisha didn't realize that someone else also stood in the room gaping at her.

"Hi Rohit, tell me!"

"Should I come later?" He winked at me and Trisha looked between the two of us.

"No, no, she is working on some graphics, tell me, we can talk." I went around the desk to speak to him.

"I needed you to review these before I put forward the plan we discussed in the morning."

I took the file from his hand to read through the changes he had made to the financial projection reports. I looked up and noticed him looking at Trisha in a daze, while she sat oblivious to him, working on the design.

"Here! Looks fine to me, now!"

He turned to look at me, took the file, and left. Before shutting the door, he glanced at her one last time, something flickering in his eyes and I didn't like it. He was my cousin, but I didn't like the way he was watching her and the way his gaze lingered on her body.

She was mine!

Mine to watch, mine to cherish, and mine to protect!

# CHAPTER EIGHT

# THE WORK TRIP

## *Trisha*

My heart leaped in joy when Viraj sprang up the surprise of a two-day visit to Jaipur but then reality sank in. Travelling alone with him, would it be, okay? What would I tell at home, dad was surely not going to like it and Ana would be stuck home alone with him?

It had been more than two months since I had started working with Viraj and after a couple of times early on, he had behaved like a gentleman, always caring, always asking my opinion, always being gentle and nowadays he often asked if I ate my food, if he could drop me home to which I would politely decline, reminding him that I used my bike to commute.

Something had changed in him, after that day when he had held my hand, he had been raging mad when Yuvraj had showed up at my desk but he didn't take the rage out on me, as I feared. He had held my hand to draw what he wanted but then his touch had gentled down as well, it wasn't the pinch of rage, it was the caress of tenderness.

And his touch so light, so gentle had evoked a deep fire of desire and awakening within me. I had never felt like this with Alok. It was wrong, oh so wrong to let him touch me even if briefly, and to not yell at him because I was with Alok, but in his defense, he had no idea. I had felt guilty and ashamed that night when I lay down on bed to sleep and remembered his touch and couldn't recall how Alok's touch made me feel even when I raked my brain.

But something had changed in him as well after that, he was more restrained, more careful with me and he talked gently and softly, often sharing titbits from his life and I had found myself opening up a little to him too. I was no more scared of him than I had been initially and I looked forward to spending time with him designing, listening to his ideas, and seeing him work. His focus and his zeal for perfection drove me to the edge wanting to outperform myself every single day.

Last week he surprised me when he asked me to stay back late and help him finish the catalog. He next proceeded to order dinner for both of us and asked what I wanted to eat.

"I can eat anything, whatever you want!"

"Then today you will eat my favourites!" He laughed making me feel warm within.

This morning, he walked into the office and called out,

"Trisha, catch this!"

I looked up and my reflexes caught whatever box he had flicked at me. I looked down to realize it was a box of Lindt chocolates. Those were the most amazing Swiss chocolates I had tasted once in college.

"What is this?"

"Someone met me downstairs and gave this. I don't eat chocolate!"

"But?"

"Yuvi said your sister loves chocolates, give it to her, if you don't want."

But I wanted!

I stood frozen in my spot at his comment while he went inside his cabin whistling softly. He remembered Yuvi mentioning that my sister loves chocolates. Seriously, was I to believe this after I had mentioned last week that chocolates were my weakness?

"Hey!" He stood leaning at his car, near the main road near my house. He had insisted on picking me up for the airport and had come in his chauffeur-driven car. He looked handsome even in a casual dark blue denim and black t-shirt. I rarely saw him in anything other than his three-piece suits.

"Hi!" He took the small bag I was carrying from my hand, opened the car door for me, and went behind to put the bag in the boot before climbing in from the other side.

"All good at home? Will your dad and sister be able to manage without you?"

"Let's hope so!"

He smiled and started discussing his plan for the next two days as the driver swiftly drove us towards the Mumbai airport.

"Do you want to see the city around?"

"No, no, we are going to work, will do that." I so wanted to see the city but was scared of saying it out loud to him.

He watched me with an intensity that threatened to burn me. He often looked at me for long, stared in fact and he still often followed me home, in his car. He kept a good distance but I knew when he was following me, and he only came till the road turning into my lane. I never asked him, because I knew he would deny or lie to my face and I didn't want that. I was starting to feel his presence around me more often now, as if my senses were tuned in and picked up whenever he watched me, even from afar.

I turned to look at him, only to realize his gaze fixated on the blue stone bangle I was wearing in my right hand. I wore a short navy blue top and light blue jeans today for travel. He had some obsession with me, every time I wore any bangles, he made it a point to touch them sometimes openly, sometimes under the pretext of handing over something to me. Every time I wore Indian traditional suits to work, he stared at me longer and harder. I impulsively flicked my wrist making the bangle jerk slightly and his hand reached out to touch it. He grazed a finger over the bangle not touching my skin at all until he looked up and realized me watching him. He pulled his hand back and smiled sheepishly.

"Why do like bangles so much?"

"Not just any, only your bangles!"

"Huh? Why?"

"I don't know, I just like them on your wrist. What do you think, I go around looking at every girl's hand for bangles?"

"How would I Know?" I laughed.

"You should know, Trisha! You are the only one!"

"Huh? What do you mean?" I asked as I dreaded his response. Hadn't he already said it all?

The car stopped, we had reached the airport and he turned to get down, without answering me. He picked up both of our bags and navigated me toward the check-in counters.

What did he mean by you are the only one? What was he hinting at? I was lost in my thoughts and didn't realize that he had completed the check-in and was now giving me my boarding pass for the security check. I looked around confused, it was the first time I was going to fly and I was lost inside the airport, not knowing what to do next.

"Take this and go through that metal detector and into that cabin, a lady will check you and stamp your boarding pass. Come out that side, I will meet you there!" He understood my dilemma and guided me. I was glad that he just told me everything without me feeling small for having to ask all this.

We ate a Subway sandwich before boarding the flight. He had booked Business Class tickets for us and made me sit near the window. Most of the time, he worked on the flight, while I looked out of the window in awe.

As the city light came into view from the top I gasped and turned to grab his hand in excitement.

"See this!" I tugged at his hand and he laughed leaning over to watch at the sight below. After a few moments, I realized I still held onto his hand which in my haste to show him the lights, I had pulled over my waist and he was leaning forward almost touching my body. His hot breath tickled my ear and I turned my face slightly to realize his gaze fixated on me and not the view below us.

"Viraj!" I mumbled.

"This view is far more beautiful than what you were showing me!"

The seat belt sign came on and he quickly moved back, shutting down his laptop and sitting straight for the landing. He was confusing me so much, what was he hinting at? Why was he saying all this to me now that we were alone on a trip?

I decided to put up the distance between us if he was misunderstanding my frankness to something else. I had no idea what he thought of me, but just the realization that he thought about me, that he was hinting at something all day today made me nervous and uncomfortable. I didn't want this trip to become a chore, I wanted to enjoy it too.

We reached the hotel in silence and checked into two adjacent rooms.

"Trisha, for dinner you want to go down or order room service?"

"I am not at all hungry, I think I will sleep early tonight!" I mumbled, not wanting to go down with him for dinner again.

"Have something, order a small meal in your room, and then sleep."

"Okay, good night!" I said as I entered my room and slowly shut the door.

The hotel we had checked into was super fancy and the room was big and nice with a very comfortable king-size bed. I clicked some photos and sent them to our sisters' WhatsApp group. Ana and I had never stayed in fancy hotels. Deeksha Di had stayed with Jiju after her marriage, but never in a five-star hotel like this one. I called them and showed them the room, talking about the flight experience and the beautiful city lights I had seen. I didn't mention Viraj and thankfully they both didn't ask anything either.

I changed into my pyjama shorts and top and was about to hit the bed, not in the mood to order anything to eat when I noticed a side door. I was perplexed as to where it opened. Was the hotel room like a suite, or was this another cupboard? I pulled the door but it didn't open, I pushed at it, and before realizing I jerked into another room.

Shit!

Viraj stood on the other side naked!

Shit! Shit!

I mean wearing only his grey track pants and nothing on top. Half-naked!

"Trisha?" He turned to me and took my sight in, his gaze pursued my short-clad legs, my short sleep top and slowly inched up to meet my eyes.

"Oh shit! I didn't know the door opened in your room!" I stepped back when he started walking toward me. "Why is there a door between two rooms?"

"This is called a connecting door or discrete affair door!" He chuckled.

"A what?"

"It is to let lovers sneak into each other's rooms at night while maintaining the pretence of staying in separate rooms for the world." He leaned down close to me, his face inches away from mine.

I gasped as his words sunk in and I realized what he was saying. I stepped back only to hit the door with my back. He put both his hands next to me, caging me in.

"Are you really this naïve, or pretending to, so you could discreetly come into my room?"

"I... no... I didn't know!"

He ran his fingers through my curls and rolled a handful of them around his fingers, feeling their texture. His gaze focused on my hair as he leaned in to smell my hair. That was my undoing! I had this impulsive urge to pull him close for a hug.

"Sorry for disturbing you, let me go sleep!" I said as I tried to control my emotions as they went in overdrive.

"Sleep? Sure, come on in!" He chuckled and I understood his invite.

"No, sleep in my room!"

"Okay!" He took a step towards my room.

"No, I will sleep in my room, you sleep in yours!"

"But you came to my room!" He pouted, teasing me now.

"I didn't know, it was your room!" I lowered my gaze, unable to hold his teasing gaze anymore.

"But you are still here, now that you know it is mine."

He pulled me to him suddenly and my body brushed against him, my breath hitched as I felt his heat and hardness against my soft curves. I put my hands up to push him away but they landed on his hot skin, over his muscled chest with a heart galloping beneath it. I felt as if I had stepped on a live-wire, his touch burned me.

"Viraj, please!" I stuttered.

"Please what, Trisha, you know how I feel about you, right?"

"No!"

"You don't? I am crazy for you, falling for you since the first time I laid my eyes on you. You are all I think every waking moment, every sleeping second."

"No!" I put my hand on his mouth to make him stop saying all this.

This was not right, he was falling for me, while I was with someone else. But he was not wrong, he didn't know. This whole thing was wrong, I was wrong.

"Trisha! You will be the death of me!" He groaned and kissed my hand that covered his mouth and I pulled it away shocked. He leaned forward to bring his mouth closer to mine.

"I have a boyfriend!" I blurted in panic.

He stilled then looked up.

"For real or just to keep me at bay?"

"Viraj, please. I have a boyfriend. We will get married in a few months!"

He took a deep breath and stepped back putting both his hands up in the air.

"I am sorry! I didn't know!" He blinked his eyes rapidly and his face contorted as if in deep pain.

I stood still, for the first time realizing his pain and his feelings. I found him weird but he had been smitten and falling for me all this while, now I understood his obsession, he thought he had a chance, he thought we had a chance. I felt for him, I felt guilty for not having told him earlier.

"I am sorry, I never meant to lead you on, or to..." I didn't know why I felt like apologizing to him. He had turned his back to me but the stiff back muscles showed the tension coursing through his body.

"Goodnight, please lock this door from your side. You will feel safe!"

"I feel safe with you!"

He turned on his heels and I saw pain mixed with rage on his face.

"You feel safe with me? Who are you kidding? You have always been scared of me, always on alert with me! I might be a man obsessed but am not a monster!"

"I am sorry!" I whispered.

"I will never hurt you!" His voice was strained. His eyes were devastated.

"I know!"

"I will... I will..." He paused looking at the ceiling controlling the emotions within, "Goodnight, will meet you for breakfast tomorrow!" He turned around and walked towards the desk, where his laptop was kept open.

I stood for a while, unsure of what to do. He was hurting, because of me, should I console him, or leave him alone? It was not my fault that he dreamed, I never led him on, I never gave him any indication that I had any feelings for him, then why was his pain hurting me so much? I didn't want him to hurt either.

I walked back to my room and closed the door but didn't have the heart to lock it. I knew he was a man of honour and would never take advantage of me, hell he could never hurt me like that!

The next morning, he came out of his room, looking freshly shaved and showered, but his exhausted eyes gave away the fact that he hadn't slept all night.

"Did you sleep well?" He asked softly.

I nodded, lying to him. Even I couldn't sleep till late into the night. I was feeling bad, guilty, and hurt for the pain I had caused him unknowingly.

"You didn't lock the door!" He stated.

"I trust you, Viraj!"

"You do now?" He pushed me to the wall and covered my body with his own pressing into me in the narrow corridor of the hotel. I was taken aback at the suddenness of it all but I realized even this didn't scare me at all anymore. His gaze was focussed on my lips, I knew what he wanted and I couldn't give him that.

"I trust you, Viraj! I know you will not force me, you will not kiss me, even when you have me caged in like this!" His pained gaze moved up to meet mine and he stepped back muttering something under his breath.

"I so want to, Trisha! But I can't!" He spoke and walked ahead.

We had to meet two suppliers during the day and we kept busy with work. For the first time, I saw him negotiating business deals and it was fascinating to see the way he worked. I had never been in any meeting with him, I had only seen his creative style of work, never the ruthless negotiating style of the CEO. He was calm and focussed and the way he carried himself, always put him in a commanding position and people couldn't hold their forts for long once he decided to conquer them. I felt proud that I got to work with him closely and that he was personally mentoring me as far as design was going.

As we finished our meetings and finalized the deals, he asked me softly if I trusted him. I nodded, wondering what had brought that on, suddenly. He extended his hand toward me and gestured for me to follow. Slowly, unsure where he was planning on going, I placed my faith in him, and took his hand.

What he did next was probably the best surprise I had ever had. He took us to the Amer Fort in Jaipur. I was in awe of the beautiful, majestic fort. He took me inside and I kept gawking at it in pure delight.

I clutched at his hand as we entered the famous Sheesh Mahal or the Mirror Palace, as it was called. I twirled around and he laughed.

"Oh my God, thank you so much for bringing me here!" I gushed holding his right hand in both of mine.

"Anytime!" He smiled softly. "If I knew you would enjoy this so much, I would have taken an extra day in the trip just to show you around and see this happiness on your face, Trisha!"

I smiled; this meant the world to me. No one had ever given my happiness, or my wishes so much priority in life. I was used to being happy with whatever came my way, and I never thought someone would just take time off, and plan for my happiness.

My eyes moistened at his words, at his thoughtful gesture of bringing me here and he caught my chin with his fingers.

"What's wrong?"

I shook my head feeling overwhelmed with emotions. After last night, he could have just finished work and gone back to the hotel, yet he brought me here, knowing well that I had not travelled or seen all this magnificence before. He wrapped up the work in a hurry, I felt him rushing in negotiations and looking at his watch a few times, now I understood, it was all for me. So, he could bring me here and show me this splendour. He made my day one of the best ones, quietly by just being his true self. He could have punished me, been mad at me after last night but he chose to rise above it all.

"Trisha, what's wrong? Why are you crying? What did I do?"

I shook my head as no words came out. And the dam burst open and tears flowed immediately making him panic even more. He thought he was making me cry; he was hurting me in some way. It was in fact the opposite; he was making me feel overwhelmed with happiness.

"Do you want to go out? Do I step away? I thought you were happy?"

"I am..." I nodded. Then I shocked both of us, with my next words, "Can I please hug you?"

"Huh? Yeah, sure, come here!"

He engulfed me in his arms as I wrapped my hands behind his back holding onto his shoulders, I hid my face in his chest and cried. I do not know why I felt so overwhelmed. I was ecstatic for one moment and his thoughtful gesture was my undoing. He kept stroking my hair softly, whispering soothing words in my ear.

"I am sorry!" I looked at his worried face as my tears stopped.

"What happened? What did I do?"

"You made me feel so cherished, Viraj. No one ever has done such a thing for me, no one ever has even thought of changing their plans based on my wishes, making new ones just to see happiness on my face. Guess your words just undid me."

He frowned, panic leaving his eyes but concern settling in.

"Oh, Trisha!" He pulled me back in a hug and I put my arms around him one more time. "Feeling better?"

I nodded, my head buried in his chest, in his amazing musky scent. I took a deep whiff and filled my senses with his warmth. The very next moment I felt guilty. He said he was obsessed with me last night, I told him I had a boyfriend and here I was giving him hope, breathing in his scent, what the heck was wrong with me?

I stepped back impulsively and he jerked his hands away surprised.

"Sorry, I cried all over you!" I said trying to hide my embarrassment. I touched the wet spot on his t-shirt where my tears had soaked him up and he gazed down at it.

"Anytime for you Trisha!"

"I am sorry for last night!"

"You lied about the boyfriend?" He teased.

"No! Not that, I mean you... I didn't know... I never meant to give you false hope..."

"Shhh..." He put a finger on my lips, and I stilled, "You didn't, it's all on me, don't worry about it at all. What I feel for you is not your fault! And I am not sorry for feeling what I feel for you!"

I looked at him with surprise, he had no resentment over this at all. He was glad he had this fetish for me even when I couldn't reciprocate his feelings or nothing could come out of it. How? Why?

I had thought he would be sad, heartbroken, and angry at me!

"I am sad, I am heartbroken but angry with you, I am not! Like I said, you are not at fault, no one is. It's all on me, and hopefully, I will get over it!"

I realized I had spoken the last words out loud, because his answer stumped me, leaving me baffled.

"Trisha, nothing changes between us, okay? I understand you have a boyfriend and I will respect that but anytime you need anything, I am here for you!" He whispered and made his way to my heart, warming me up to his charisma, one more time.

The rest of our trip was uneventful and a lot of fun. Once, he was not hiding what he felt, he opened up and was a fun guy to hang around with and I found myself sharing with him, laughing, and teasing him too. On our flight back, I was tired and fell asleep, only to wake up and realize I was using his shoulder as my pillow. He had sat through the flight, not moving, not working lest it disturb my sleep.

"Oh, I am so sorry! Why didn't you wake me up?"

"It's okay, I didn't mind it."

"But you couldn't work, what did you do?"

"Watched you!"

A shiver ran down my spine. His obsession didn't seem to die at all.

"Relax, I was reading on my Kindle!" He laughed, "Look at your face, you think am some sort of a pervert or psycho?"

"Hi" I hugged Alok when I met him over the weekend. We were yet again at his flat and yet again the pizza sat awaiting me. I told him about my Jaipur trip and he frowned.

"So, you went alone with Viraj?"

"Yeah, I had told you right, he is working on launching a collection, which is entirely his own."

"Then what are you doing in that?"

"Designing with him!"

"You are talking as if you are his partner or something, I don't like the sound of any of this!"

I didn't understand what the problem was, I had told him, I was working as his assistant designer, I had told him before going to Jaipur that I was travelling with Viraj for work.

"What do you not like?"

"Why is Viraj working so closely with you?"

I gulped, Alok would completely lose his shit if he knew Viraj's feelings for me, or how he made me work from his cabin.

"He needs an assistant and I am perfect because I do not have much experience, so he can mold my working style to his own."

"Stay away from that man, he is a man-whore. I don't want him to try his charms on you!"

My heart flipped in my chest, Viraj, man-whore? He didn't seem like one. In the past three months I had known him, I never once saw him partying or hanging around with anyone.

I slowly shifted the topic off Viraj because that was making me uncomfortable. I was hiding things from Alok and I didn't like it. Viraj and I were forming a new friendship, even when I knew what he felt for me, but I felt safe with him. Alok would not understand that. We girls had a special radar, we could identify various touches and people's vibes.

I was sitting at the design desk in Viraj's cabin trying colour options for the finalized designs, when the door burst open.

"Viraj, I think..." I paused when I realized it wasn't Viraj but Rohit, his cousin who had walked in.

"Hi, I am Rohit!"

"Hi, I know you. I am Trisha."

"What are you doing here?"

"I was working on these designs, Viraj is in a meeting."

"What is going on between you two?"

"Huh? Nothing!"

"Viraj has always been a loner, working alone, especially when it came to his designs. Are you sleeping with him?"

"No!" I blurted shocked at his accusation.

"Rohit?" Viraj's curt voice reached me before I could see his face.

Rohit stilled for a second before turning to face Viraj.

"How come you are here?" Viraj's tone was sweet, he had not heard what his brother just accused me of.

"Excuse me!" I said and rushed out from there.

"I was wondering if we could have lunch together and maybe you could fill me on your Jaipur trip!" I heard Rohit say to Viraj as I closed the cabin door behind me.

# CHAPTER NINE

# THE ACCIDENT

## *Viraj*

I paused and looked up to see her frowning in concentration at the fabric that she was trying to drape around for her new dress idea. I loved watching her work, I loved watching her, period. Anything she did, enticed me. I should have backed off when she said she had a boyfriend, and though I never touched her or pressed her to spend more time with me, my feelings had not changed for her if anything they had only intensified.

I was still as obsessed with her as I was on the day she had walked in for the interview, I still stalked her and drove behind her till she turned into her lane on her bike, only then did I return home every night. I watched her from the half-open blinds when she sat at her desk working or chatting with any of the other employees. I watched her every morning, as she brewed two cups of coffee, one for me, one for herself.

I watched her in my sleep, in my dreams too. My sketchbook with her sketches had only become thick over the past four months that she had been working with me. Almost every day she gave me a memory that was so clearly etched on my mind that I replicated it on paper at night, sitting late at my desk.

I felt someone was choking me to death when she uttered that she had a boyfriend, that was my worst fear coming true. And I couldn't sleep a wink that night, I had drawn her face, her worried eyes which called to my soul on sheets of paper I found in the notepad at the hotel room. I had watched her slip away from my reach and I couldn't do a thing.

The next day when she hugged me, I wanted the time to still, the earth to just stop rotating, so I could have her in my arms forever but alas, she stepped away as soon as she was able to compose herself.

She was such a gentle, pure soul, why had no one made her smiles, or her wishes a priority? What would I not do to spend a lifetime bringing her smiles, making her eyes light up in joy every second of the day? But I couldn't. Who was her boyfriend? Shouldn't he be the one bringing her those joys, what was that idiot doing if not treating her like a queen? I had just mentioned if I knew she would enjoy the fort so much, I would have planned one more day stay in Jaipur, what was one day I could settle down there forever with her if she asked?

Why was such a simple thing overwhelming for her? Did no one care for her well-being at all in her family? She was working hard, earlier doing multiple jobs for the sake of her family but what about them? Were they not taking care of her?

A brief knock on the door interrupted my thoughts and I turned to see Naman, my best friend walk inside smiling.

"Hey Man!" He fist bumped me and gave me a slight side hug.

"Naman, how are you dude! Long time!"

"You are the one missing all our outings!"

I laughed. She fidgeted nervously behind and caught Naman's attention.

"Hi!" She spoke in a soft voice when she noticed both of our gaze on her.

"Trisha, this is Naman, my best friend and this is Trisha, my assistant designer, she is helping me with my new collection."

"Lovely meeting you, why do I feel I have seen you before!"

"Nice meeting you too. I used to work at the pharmacy store in Worli."

"Oh, right! The condom girl!" Naman blurted and she coughed uncomfortably.

"What?"

"Shlok sent me to the pharmacy to buy condoms for him and there she was at the counter; it was so awkward man!" Naman turned to me and I heard her giggling behind. We both turned to look at her.

"He also met me for the first time, when he was buying condoms!" She laughed.

"Not me, Shlok was buying!" I clarified.

"How many does he use everyday!" Naman asked and I rolled my eyes not wanting to go down that line of discussion.

"You got too!" She laughed looking at me, I groaned at that memory and Naman looked between the two of us.

"What would you do with the condoms? You have stopped meeting anyone since you fell in love." Naman laughed and I tensed at his words.

She frowned, her confused gaze settling on me.

Love was not the word to be used!

"Did you find that girl?" Naman suddenly asked and I looked at Trisha, shit, she was right here. I never told Naman anything but he was the observant one in our trio and he had sensed something.

"Dude, what brings you here today?" I asked him instead.

Naman understood I was changing the topic, then he looked at Trisha and settled down on the chair in front of my desk.

"I will take your leave if that's okay!" She asked me and I nodded.

"Be safe!" I said as she waved bye to Naman and left.

"What's going on?"

"Did you have to say all that in front of her?"

"Yeah, sorry I realized late. But what I said isn't wrong."

"I am obsessed with her, not in love."

"Really? Obsession going on for what almost a year now?"

"Ten months!"

"Do you remember the date you first met her?"

"Saw her, yes!"

"Seriously!" He threw both his hands up in the air.

My phone broke the banter Naman and I were having, reminiscing our college days and I turned to pick it up.

Trisha Calling...

"Hello?"

"Viraj!" She paused then she grunted and sighed heavily.

"What's wrong?"

"I need help! I have had an accident."

"Accident? Where are you?" I stood up abruptly, my entire body tensing at the word accident.

"I am not hurt much but my *Activa*, I can't walk."

"I am coming, you send me your live location."

I gestured for Naman to come along; he was also standing up waiting for me to tell what was wrong.

I told Naman that Trisha had met with an accident on our way to meet her.

She sat on the footpath, a police officer talking to her. I surveyed the injuries on her, her left foot was swollen, her left hand was bleeding so was her forehead. Naman took over immediately, talking to the police officer while I picked her up and put her in my car.

"You take her to the hospital; I will finish the formalities and get her bike to a service centre." Naman said and I nodded.

There were no broken bones but a lot of bruises on her, as she had fallen on her left side. Someone had rammed into her bike at full speed as she was slowing down for the signal and sped away. A clear hit-and-run case.

She had seen the car but not the number plate as it came from behind. Naman joined us just as she was bandaged up and we were ready to leave.

"Hit and run case! I will keep following up, are you okay?" He asked her and she nodded.

"I am sorry, I troubled you!"

"No, trouble at all." He smiled.

She slowly stood up from the bed she was on and winced as her swollen foot couldn't take her weight. Naman and I both moved toward her impulsively, he grabbed her hand while I bent and picked her up.

"Viraj!" She looked at me stunned.

"You can't walk like this!" I started walking towards the parking lot, Naman following us.

Naman made small talk as we drove to her place. For the first time in all these months, I turned the car in her lane and stopped right in front of her door. Naman and I helped her inside the house, another girl, maybe a few years younger than Trisha came running to help her.

"Di, what happened?"

"My *Activa*!" Was all Trisha said and Naman burst into laughter.

"What happened to *Dhanno*? Where is it?" Her sister's words made Naman chuckle loud. He was so enjoying this!

"This is my sister Anaisha, Yuvi's friend. And this is my boss Viraj and his friend Naman. They came to help at the accident spot." Trisha spoke glaring at her sister, Anaisha.

"Hi, please come!"

"No, we came to drop her, you take care and Trisha, I should not see you in the office for at least one week!"

"I will..."

"Shhh..." I glared at her.

We said our goodbyes and went back to our car.

"You found her!" Naman broke the silence.

"Huh?"

"You found her; Trisha is the girl you have been crazy about, right?"

"Yes!"

"Where had you seen her the first time, not while buying condom, I suppose!"

"No, I saw her 10 months back in Yuvi's college, she worked there as a Librarian but was teaching girls dance for the fest."

"Ahhh... now it makes sense! Why you were so keen on attending the fest when even Yuvi wasn't attending. Why you stopped sleeping around and why you stopped seeing us for the last four five months completely, she had started working in your office!"

I smirked. He had put everything together within a moment.

"Did you find her and give her a job or she came unaware?"

"She came in for an interview and I was shocked to see her, I spoke to her, saw her designs and they were so good that I decided to hire her, but because of who she was I hired her as my assistant instead of her joining the design team, she came to interview for!"

"So, you created a job on the fly!"

"Pretty much!"

"Smart and now you are in love!"

"I am not..."

"Who are you kidding? You are totally, completely in love with her. What about her? Does she know?"

"She has a boyfriend!"

"What the fuck, man?"

"She doesn't know I am in love with her, she knows I have been stalking her for a while now and she knows I feel something for her."

"And?"

"And nothing, she can't do a thing about how I feel and I can't do a thing about how I feel, I can't help it if even after knowing she is with someone else, my feelings for her only get intensified instead of fading away."

"Feelings don't fade away; you need to try and distance yourself from her!"

"Dude, I can't. I have to live, right!"

"Oh man!" He gruntled in frustration. He knew there was nothing that could be done for me, now.

The next two days were hard on me, not seeing her in the office left me feeling empty within, I couldn't work without her being around, I couldn't focus on the meetings. I managed not just textiles but all other companies under the Rajvansh group of Industries as well and the days and nights without her being around were painful to say the least.

On the third day, I couldn't hold myself back anymore, and landed up at her house. She sat in her living room, wearing shorts and a t-shirt, her leg stretched out as she read a novel.

"Viraj?"

"Can I come inside?"

"Yes, of course! But..." She looked around then slowly added, "No one is home."

I paused at the threshold.

"I came to see you, are you better?"

"Yeah, see the swelling is all gone!" She extended her leg towards me and all I saw was miles and miles of skin on her long legs, my body going in a frenzy.

"I should go now; do you need anything?"

"Why, come inside."

"No one is home, I don't want you to land in any trouble. I wanted to see you and I have seen you!" And have seen your shapely bare legs, now these would haunt me at night. I groaned at the image that was imprinted on my mind now.

"No, there won't be any trouble, please come!"

I slowly stepped inside and saw her small house oozing with warmth and beautifully decorated with mostly handmade stuff. Nothing fancy, nothing sophisticated, but all made by the family with their own hands for their house.

It was a Sunday afternoon and surprisingly the entire family was at the huge dining table we had at home enjoying the hot lunch.

"Viraj beta, this Friday evening keep yourself free, we have to attend an engagement party and you must come with us." My mom said from across the table.

"I will try!" I grunted non-committal.

I was not keeping any of my evenings free for someone's engagement I personally didn't know of.

"Deepanita will also be there, we want you both to meet!"

I paused eating and looked up.

"Who?"

"Deepanita, she is beautiful. Khanna ji and we were thinking of arranging your marriage with her!" Dad supplied.

Yuvraj whistled next to me and Kaki ma, chastised him.

"I don't need anyone arranging my marriage. I am busy enough, when I want to marry, I will."

"Busy with what? You are of age, and then there are other kids waiting behind you!" Mom exclaimed.

"Busy with my life, with my career. And who is asking anyone else to wait? They are more than welcome to marry and settle down if they want."

"Oh, I am so ready!" Yuvi grinned and earned a smack on his head from me.

"Yuvi, shut up. Enough of your dodging our attempts, Viraj. If you have someone, let us know or else we will fix up your wedding." My dad ordered.

"I won't marry just because you are fixing it up and no, I don't have anyone."

"But you do, Bhai!" Rohit blurted and I looked up sharply. Mom dropped her spoon dramatically while Kaki ma glared at her son.

"Who is it, Rohit?" My dad asked.

"A new assistant, Trisha. Bhai is trying to woo. She is always beside him." I groaned in disgust. Idiot had to blurt her name here!

"Bhai?" Yuvi looked up horrified and I groaned all over again.

"Shut up Rohit. She is just an assistant; I am not trying to woo her or anything else."

"Oh, then can I have her?" Rohit smirked.

"Rohit!"

"Bhaiya!"

Yuvraj and I both glared at him and everyone else looked at us both confused. I looked at Yuvi and gestured for him to follow me and we both walked out of the dining room.

"Bhai?"

"Relax, nothing is going on between me and Trisha. She has a boyfriend; I am just working with her on a brand-new collection I am trying to design individually and hence we work together."

"Bhai, don't hurt her!"

"Why do you think I will hurt her?"

"No, you won't but she is too special and you know it too."

I nodded. I couldn't admit to him how special she was to me! I would hurt the entire world if needed for her but hurting her was out of the question.

"How do you know she has a boyfriend when Ana and I have no clue?"

I looked up alarmed, shucks, I didn't mean to spill her beans.

"She once mentioned, she is planning on getting married to him soon!"

"Interesting, how is Ana not aware?"

"Maybe Ana is and only you are not."

"No chance!"

"Is Ana your... I mean you and Ana?"

"No! No, not at all."

I frowned, was there something brewing there too that he was hiding from me, how I was hiding from him about Trisha?

# CHAPTER TEN

# FACE TO FACE WITH REALITY

## *Viraj*

Monday morning, I reached Trisha's house to take her to the office. To say she was surprised was an understatement. Her *Activa* was still at the service center and last I checked it would take time to repair it fully.

"Why did you come? I was just about to take an auto." She was dressed and ready to go back to work.

"Auto? Why? I am at your service!"

"Why? Why are you wasting your time?"

"I am spending time with you, how is that a waste?" I took her bag from her hand and extended my hand to help her sit in my car but she shook her head.

We drove to the office and I asked if she needed help walking upstairs and she glared at me horrified.

"No! Don't even ask, people are already spinning tales, I can't be seen coming and going with you!"

"Spinning tales? What? Did someone say anything to you?"

She paused in her tracks absolutely quiet.

"Trisha?"

"No, just office gossip!"

"Who?"

"Nothing! Come."

"Trisha, I won't move from here until you tell me who said what to you?"

She looked conflicted.

"Promise me you won't say a word to him. You won't punish him."

I stayed quiet.

"Promise me, else I won't say a word."

"Okay, fine! Promise."

"Rohit!"

"What did he say?"

I gritted, yesterday he blabbered in front of my parents, and now this.

"He asked me if I was..." She looked uncomfortable, hiding her gaze from me, "if I was sleeping with you!" She blurted and I froze.

What the heck!

Rohit surely had a death wish. I stormed towards the lift.

"Viraj, you promised! You promised me you won't!" She grabbed my hand to turn me to face her. "Won't you keep your promise?"

"I would keep every single promise I make to you but not this. How? How am I supposed to stay quiet after hearing how he insulted you, Trisha?"

"Promise is a promise. You won't say a word or punish him. Please let it be."

I gave in to her demands and agreed not to do a thing for now, but I would keep a closer eye on him and try such that he was never alone with Trisha to say anything vile.

She knocked at the door of my cabin and walked in, when I gestured for her to come, I was on a phone call and she quietly went to the design desk. I liked this about her, she was very quiet when she noticed I was on a call or working on something else, she tried to blend into the background, not realizing that I noticed her breathing as well. Today she wore a light pink shirt, my favourite colour now, especially on her with a black trouser. She was always smartly dressed but very modest and conservative. She stood arranging something on the desk, probably new designs for me to review, when I finished my call and walked toward to her.

A strand of her luscious hair fell forward on her face and she jerked her head towards the left to move it away but to no avail. I stood watching her mesmerized. How can such simple gestures steal my breath? She jerked her head again but the hair strand stayed where it was. I impulsively reached for it, and tugged it behind her left ear, my finger softly brushing her petal soft skin and she froze. A sizzle passed through me and I realized I shouldn't have touched her.

She looked up, her grey eyes beckoning me to sin but I had to control my urges and not give in. She wasn't mine to behold.

"New designs?" I asked focusing my gaze on the sketches laid out on the desk.

"Yeah, what do you think of these?"

I gestured for her to sit and I pulled another chair to sit beside her and focus on the designs and not her. She managed to undo me, even now when I knew she wasn't mine, and probably never would be.

The week went by quite beautifully as I picked her up and dropped her back every day of the week, though she kept protesting. I was having the time of my life, I was getting to spend a few extra hours with her, that too outside the office in a relaxed environment.

We were on our way to the office on Friday morning when my phone rang. A French brand of clothing I had been pursuing for a while, for partnership was in Mumbai and the gentleman wanted to meet me. I spoke to him and we decided to meet him for dinner at the Oberoi Hotel where he was staying.

"Trisha, I want you to come along, we need to meet this prospective business partner, if this guy agrees, I will launch this collection of mine in collaboration with their brand."

"Me? What will I do there?"

"Please, come along, in case he wants to look at some designs as well."

Trisha was nervous to meet the prospective client because today she was dressed in jeans and a floral top, and she felt she would not look presentable. Oh, my angel you would look presentable even in a rag!

I stopped at a western clothes boutique, I had taken Vandana to at times and bought her a dark blue chic blazer to wear on her jeans and top. It suited her well. She fidgeted when it came to paying for it but I told her it was a gift from me because I was the one making her go at such short notice. She kept arguing but I was having none of it.

Our dinner went very well and Mr. Charles agreed to work in collaboration with me. He suggested that I launch this as my collection outside of the Rajvansh Group of Industries label because RGI had a reputation and a marketplace to cater to already. If I went solo on this collection, we could really break free of that baggage and we could experiment better with trends and designs. I had myself been thinking about this for a while and when he validated my thinking it made complete business sense.

Now, I just had to convince my dad and my uncle that I was going to launch a solo collection in collaboration with Mr. Charles's brand and not Rajvansh Group. I was prepared to face resistance from my dad, he wouldn't like it, my uncle might understand this better and there was a possibility that he would support me on this.

We stepped out of the restaurant in the Oberois and she twirled around looking at the interiors and I slowed further down watching her child-like glee.

"Do you want to see their rooms?"

"Why?" She looked at me like I had lost all my marbles.

"Relax, I am not taking you to a room, just a tour, to see, not to stay."

"No, no. I don't want that."

As we approached the main reception area, she slowed down in front of a banquet hall reading the board. The banquet hall was decorated with white and purple flowers.

## *Welcome to the engagement of*

## *Alok Bansal with Priyanka Garg*

"Alok Bansal with Priyanka Garg. I know these guys; come I will wish them quickly and we can go home." I spoke when she kept standing frowning at the door.

"Trisha?" I touched her elbow and she jumped, "What happened?"

"What were you saying?"

"I said, I know both the guy and the girl, let me quickly wish them and then we will go home, if it is okay with you?"

"Yeah, sure."

We stepped inside the banquet hall and a lavish party was going on with loud music and lots of champagne.

I walked up to the stage where the bride and the groom stood and congratulated them, realizing only now that this must have been the party my mom wanted me to attend. It also meant the girl she wanted me to meet would be around and I needed to step out before being spotted by anyone.

I saw my mom standing in one corner talking to three other ladies and I needed to just turn around and walk out of here. I had come, I had wished the new couple, and now nothing else mattered. Moreover, Trisha would be getting late too, it was past 10 already now and she would be waiting for me outside. I decided to take my leave from the couple.

Suddenly, Alok's face went pale and I saw shock registering and he was splashed with a full glass of red wine. The dude was wearing a white suit for his engagement and the stain, I cringed at the thought.

I turned to see, who had done this and to my horror, Trisha stood next to me with the empty glass in her hand.

"Trish!" Alok spoke and she raised her hand to slap him hard.

"Let's go now!" She said to me.

The next moment she turned around and started walking out leaving Alok, Priyanka, and me absolutely stunned. I was horrified, what just happened? Why did she barge in like that, throw a glass of red wine, slap him, and now was walking out of the hall with me rushing after her?

Then everything clicked in place. Alok knew her, he called her Trish.

Her boyfriend!

Oh shit!

I ran to catch up with her.

"Where?" She asked looking around frustrated when she couldn't locate the exit.

"Come!" I entwined her fingers with mine and marched towards the exit.

We got in the car, quietly and started on our way back.

"He was?" I asked just to be sure I wasn't assuming things.

"My boyfriend I told you, I have one, right!" Her voice was wobbly but she was holding strong. "Bastard is getting married to a rich babe."

"They are childhood sweethearts! I know them... I wish I had asked you who your boyfriend was but I thought it wasn't my place!"

She closed her eyes and sighed deeply. I wanted to gather her in my arms and comfort her.

"Do you want me to stop the car, at the side?"

"No, no keep going. Now, I guess I don't have a boyfriend!" She replied flatly.

My heart leaped in joy only to crash back into a million pieces looking at her face contorted in pain. She was trying too hard to hold it together. I drove to her home quietly, glancing at her profile from time to time. She had her eyes shut tight holding the tsunami of tears in, I was sure because her face told the state of her heart. She was broken, she was hurting but not letting it show. We reached her locality and I stopped in front of her house.

"Trisha!"

She slowly opened her eyes and looked at me.

"We have reached!"

She looked around as if in a daze then saw her house and nodded.

"Thanks!" She got down slowly from the car, I had never seen her look so hassled and disoriented. She was usually always in control.

She took a few steps inside the veranda and instead of opening the door, like she always did, she slowly turned to the stairs that went all the way up to the terrace. I saw her climb up slowly and I drove out of her lane. I parked my car in a parallel lane which was broader than hers and ran back to her building, it was deserted and quiet.

Slowly I inched my way up the stairs only to find her sitting on the terrace in a dark corner. She was howling her pain out by covering her mouth with her hands so no noise came out. In the moonlight, I saw her flowing tears and her dishevelled hair. She had surely pulled at them.

I felt searing pain spread through me seeing her plight. Why was I feeling this heaviness, this pain? I wanted to rush up to her and gather her into my arms. I wanted to tell her that I was here for her, that she wasn't alone. I wanted to tell her that Alok didn't deserve her but I did none of these. I stood in the dark shadows and watched her cry incessantly. She didn't shed a single tear when she was in the car, she didn't want me to see her in this state. She didn't want me to see her helplessness, her heart break and I would keep her wish.

I would never mention that I saw her breaking apart, I would never tell her that I saw her in a weak moment if she didn't want me to.

I stood in the shadows for a long time, long enough for my girl to wipe all her tears, for her to chin up and take a deep breath. My tigress was ready to face the world. I hoped she was because seeing her so broken, so exhausted made me feel a new kind of helplessness that I had never felt before and I didn't like the feel of it.

She slowly stood up, dusted her clothes, picked up her bag, and walked towards the terrace door, straight towards where I was hiding. I moved further back into the shadows; I didn't have time to run down the stairs because she could see me. I stood still and I think I even stopped breathing for a few seconds, as she stepped out and without looking back, just walked down the stairs. I climbed after her and noticed her entering her house and shutting the door behind her.

I stayed put for a few minutes and then sneaked out undetected.

# CHAPTER ELEVEN

# Facing the Reality

**Trisha**

I got down from the car absolutely lost and I felt a crushing pain, I needed to bleed this pain out else it would choke me. On an impulse I went up to the terrace, at night, the terrace of our house was my safe haven, no one ever came here. And I always found solace in the fresh air and under the moonlit sky.

When my mother had died, this was where I had come every night to shed my tears, wipe them, and hide them from the rest of the family to put up a brave front, and that is what I had done tonight too. I couldn't believe my eyes as Viraj had walked up the stage, my gaze had followed him.

There on the stage stood Alok, my boyfriend of the past four years looking happy and dapper in a white suit with a purple tie with his new fiancée dressed in a long flowy purple gown looking like a princess. My legs automatically took me towards him and I had no idea what I wanted to ask or say to him until a waiter crossed me with a tray filled with wine and champagne glasses. I just picked one and I knew how I wanted to break up with him.

He looked so happy holding his fiancée's hand and laughing with Viraj and other guests that my whole body burned with rage. His gaze fixated on me the moment he saw me climb up the stage. I saw fear cross his eyes as I inched closer to him. He was not expecting me at the party tonight. Damn, he had even asked me to come to his house the next day, would he have told me the truth or continued living the dual life?

I threw whatever was in the glass on his face and it soaked his suit coat and shirt. He dared to call me Trish and I slapped him hard, only those who loved me called me that, not everyone got that privilege. I just turned around to walk out.

I was so glad when I felt Viraj rushing out after me. I was not alone for just this once. I wanted to give in to my impulse of breaking apart knowing Viraj would gather my broken pieces, but I couldn't even let go. I just felt numb with the pain, he guided me out of the wretched hotel and into his car. He told me that Alok was getting married to his childhood sweetheart and I felt someone had stabbed my heart with a dagger.

If she was his childhood sweetheart, what the hell was I? What was he planning to do with me? Keep me as his side chick? His mistress? Bile rose in my mouth and I shook my head to rid myself of all the thoughts. I closed my eyes to keep the tears at bay. I was on the verge of falling apart but I was not used to showing my vulnerability to anyone and I had waited to be alone, waited till Viraj was gone.

I was glad Viraj brought me home, and I knew he stood in the shadows watching me cry on the terrace but didn't come any closer. I needed to be alone, I couldn't have cried if he had come over. The moment I realized he stood at the door, in the dark shadows, I wiped my tears and prepared myself that he would come barging in, asking me to not cry, asking me to be strong, telling me it wasn't my fault, and consoling me. But he won over a piece of my shattered heart when he did nothing of the sort and stood quietly in the shadows, watching over me from a distance.

I sat waiting for a while and sighed in relief when I realized he was there yet not coming over to me. I cried then in relief, I howled my pain out, to empty my heart of all the feelings I had for Alok, to rid myself of his memories and when I felt a little better and collected, I gathered myself, because that is what I always did.

I knew this pain would linger for a long time, the pain of heartbreak, the pain of loss, and the pain of betrayal but I had to go on. I would not let that asshole Alok screw my life anymore. I had my blessings and I was so glad I went to the hotel for that meeting today and managed to see his deception with my own eyes. And somewhere I was glad I ruined his suit and his evening with his new fiancée. I am sure there would have been questions asked at the party after I pulled my stunt and left the party in haste.

I wiped my tears and got up slowly, giving time for Viraj to rush back downstairs but he still stood there in the shadows as I purposefully ignored him and walked down the stairs. If he thought I didn't know of his presence, I would give him that. He gave me the solitude that I so needed yet watched over me.

Saturday went by in almost a daze, Ana's friend was coming home to study together with her and I asked if Ana could go to her house instead, faking a headache and Ana left soon after. Dad as usual was nowhere to be found and I spent the day alone, destroying and trashing every single thing Alok had ever given to me. Late in the evening, I saw a message from Viraj asking if I was, okay. I replied that I would be, very soon. There was no hiding from him, he had seen me breaking apart, he had seen the entire thing unfold right in front of his eyes.

On Sunday afternoon, Viraj showed up at my doorstep, dressed in a striped white and dark blue t-shirt and light blue denim jeans.

"Hi!"

"I couldn't stay back anymore, I needed to see you to be sure, you were okay!" The concern in his voice and the worry in his eyes made something within me melt.

"I am better, thanks! Come on in." I stepped back to let him inside. I was wearing my old track pants and t-shirt at home, and I was sure he thought I looked like a beggar.

Ana came out of the room and paused when she saw Viraj at the door.

"Hi!"

"Hi Ana, how are you?"

"Good! How are you?"

"I am good, thanks!"

I went into the kitchen to make tea for him when I felt his presence behind me.

"Trisha, take a couple of days off if you need it?"

"No! I think work will keep me occupied and my mind off all this."

"Are you sure? You look so tired and..." He brushed his thumb gently under my eye. I knew I had dark circles; I had been crying and not sleeping since Friday evening.

"Viraj! I am sorry for Friday!" I blurted.

"For what? I should be saying sorry, if I had not gone in to wish them, you wouldn't have to see them."

"No, actually thanks for that!" I cut him short. "I am glad you went in to wish them and I saw the reality with my eyes and now I know better. I am sorry for what I did that day. Throwing champagne on him, slapping him, then stomping out of the room, that's not me."

"Wine! That was red wine. And that exactly is what made me feel so proud of you! I know how devastated you were but you flipped him in style."

"And then completely broke apart!" I sighed. He stayed silent. "I know you were watching over me as I sat crying on the terrace. Thanks for being there and extending your silent support! It meant a lot!"

"I will always be there if you would let me and I really wish, I never have to witness you falling apart like that ever in my life!"

Tears spilled out of my eyes yet again and he slowly wiped them.

"It's okay to cry sometimes, Trisha, just let it all out!"

I nodded as tears flowed down freely from my eyes.

"I am here if you need a hug or want to use my t-shirt to wipe your tears!"

I laughed suddenly at his words and he pulled me in a hug holding me close until I composed myself and dried my tears on his t-shirt.

"Better?"

I stepped back only to realize Ana was standing at the kitchen door horrified.

"Ana?"

"What's wrong? Why are you crying?" She stood rooted in her spot.

"I think you both need to talk and I will get going!" Viraj whispered. "Share Trisha, at times that's what's needed!"

"Have some tea!"

"Some other time!" He pecked my forehead and walked out, patting Ana's head softly and bending down to whisper in her ears, "Take care of your sis for me, please!"

She looked at him confused then nodded.

I told Ana everything from the start and she was furious on my behalf.

"Why didn't you tell me earlier?"

"I didn't want to burden you!"

"But Di, would you not hope that if this happened with me, I would come and tell you, first thing and not confide in an almost stranger, Viraj or someone else?"

"I never confided anything; he was there. He saw it unfolding, unfortunately!"

"I am glad he was there to get you out of that place and back home safe. I am so glad he came to check on you today as well. Why do I have a feeling that he has feelings for you?"

"He has!"

"He does?" She looked at me surprised and I nodded.

"Yes, but I had told him I had a boyfriend and he backed off."

"Oh my God, does Yuvi know?"

"I don't know! Please, Ana, don't utter a word to Yuvi, I don't know what their equation is!"

"You are right! I won't."

My *Activa* was not yet repaired and when I stepped out of my house on Monday morning to get to the office, I saw his car parked and he waited inside patiently.

"When did you come?"

"A while back, I was sure, you would try to leave early and sneak without me!"

"Viraj, I am not used to so much pampering!"

"Then get used to it, because this is what I intend to do always!"

I froze at his words and he stilled too.

"For as long as you would let me be around you Trisha! I am not asking for anything from you in return, I am not seeking a chance just because Alok is now out of the scene. Nothing has changed for me."

I stayed quiet not because I didn't want to say anything, I wanted to but I didn't know what to say, what to tell him. I couldn't think of giving him a chance, not so soon after the heartbreak. I didn't trust anyone right now, Viraj had been good to me, caring for me like no one else, but I didn't love him.

I loved Alok who had betrayed me so badly, and now I doubted my capability of falling in love ever again. Would I be able to trust anyone after Alok? I gave him my heart, my trust, four long years, and look where he got me!

I sat at the design desk trying to sketch and failing miserably. Viraj had left me alone since after lunchtime and gone on to have his meetings outside. He had ordered two plates of food, when I told him that I had no desire to eat, and forced me to eat with him, before leaving for his meeting.

Suddenly, the door burst open and two men walked in laughing only to freeze at my sight. I recognized Naman immediately who smiled warmly at my sight but the other guy frowned looking at me.

"Hey Trisha, how are you? All your injuries healed?" Naman came forward to hug me from the side and I was surprised at his action.

"I am fine, thanks! How are you?"

"All good!" He spread his hands as if letting me see that he was all good. I liked this man; he was always happy and jovial unlike his grumpy friend Viraj.

"This is Shlok, our third friend, and Shlok, this is Trisha, Viraj's assistant designer."

"Hi!" Shlok shook my hand. "Viraj is on his way here, so we decided to wait for him here."

"Sure, please sit. I will be outside!" I quickly cleaned up the desk and started to move out.

I was about to open the door when someone opened it from outside and it hit me square in the face. I whimpered in pain.

"Shit! Not again. I am so sorry!" Viraj held my face in his palms and pressed hard over my hand. Naman stood next to me checking as well.

"Not again?" Shlok asked looking confused at the scene in front of him.

"I banged the door at her face once before as well," Viraj spoke and turned to me, "Let me see Trish, move your hand!"

I froze, did he just call me Trish? He realized his folly and looked at Naman, who put an arm around my shoulder and took me back to the desk rubbing my forehead.

"Are you okay?" Naman whispered.

I nodded feeling a small bump on my forehead.

"Why do you get hurt every single time we meet?" He laughed.

"Right! You are never meeting her again!" Viraj declared and Shlok rolled his eyes.

I laughed and took their leave, leaving the friends together to catch up on whatever they had come for. Naman was overtly warm towards me today and protective of me in some strange manner, had Viraj told him something?

All three of them walked out of the cabin about an hour later and waved bye to me and Rajni, who was preparing to leave as well. Viraj didn't go with them but instead saw them off in the elevator.

"I can leave when you are ready!"

"I will go on my own!"

"No, not happening."

"Alright, I need 10 minutes."

"Just come over when you are ready!" He gestured toward his room and walked back inside.

He drove me back home quietly, lost in his thoughts and I didn't ask him anything either. As he stopped the car in front of my house, I saw my dad standing at the door. I panicked seeing him there, mumbled a bye, and rushed out of the car.

"Baba?"

"Who was he? Where are you coming from?" Baba raised his voice.

Baba was surprisingly not drunk today but that also meant he was in a foul mood.

"He was my boss because it was late, he came to drop, come inside Baba." I turned to see that the car had left, I sighed in relief and pulled my dad inside the house.

"Boss, are you coming back from the office?"

"Yes!"

"Why is your boss dropping you home? Are you now doing extra work for him?"

"Baba!"

"No, tell me, look in my eyes, are you sleeping around with your boss?"

"No!"

"Then do that, he seemed rich, ask him for money!"

"Baba!"

"I know you are good for nothing, might as well earn some money from him! Sleep with him, he will throw money at you. I need money for my drinks, I am in debt."

The door burst open and Viraj stood seething fire.

Damn it, why was he here?

"Viraj?" I said but my voice came out a pained whisper.

"Your daughter works in my company and I will not tolerate anyone talking shit about her."

I pushed Viraj out of the house.

"I am so sorry, he is drunk, please leave!"

"I came to give you this," He lifted his hand which carried my stole, I must have forgotten it in his car in my rush and he came back to give it to me when he overheard some parts of the conversation.

"Thanks!"

"What was going on? Is he your dad?"

I looked down at the floor, at his black leather shoes to be precise. I couldn't meet his gaze.

"Are you rich? Do you like her?" The door burst open yet again and my dad asked Viraj.

I tugged at his hand shaking my head.

"Please go! I am so sorry!"

"Trish?" He was worried for me, "I won't leave you alone here."

"He is my father. Please go, I don't want you witnessing any more ugliness of my life." I almost pushed him out of the veranda and he drove away looking at me with worry-filled eyes.

# CHAPTER TWELVE

# Taking Things in My Hands

## *Viraj*

I couldn't believe a father could talk like that to his daughter. She had rushed out of my car and forgot her stole. I noticed after coming out of her lane, so I turned around and went back to hand it over to her and get one more glimpse of her, but before I could knock on her door, the agitated voice from inside reached me and I heard something that she would not have wanted me to hear in a million years.

She felt guilt, she was ashamed of what I had heard, but why was she ashamed, her father should have felt that emotion. It took all of my restraint to not knock the old man down and leave her alone with him that night.

"Naman, I need help!" I dialled my most trusted man for what I had in my mind.

"Tell me!"

"I need you to use that investigation agency and find out all the history and background of Trisha and her father!"

"Trisha? Why now?"

"Her father I think abuses her."

"What?"

"I heard him asking her to sleep with me and earn extra money for his liquor!"

"Shit man!"

"Yeah!"

"I will get started on this and will have a report ASAP."

"Thanks, buddy!"

"Viraj..."

"Yeah?"

"Isn't that what you want?"

"I want a forever with her, not just sleep and throw money at her."

"Thought so was just double checking!" He chuckled and I laughed, he had made me smile even when I was worried for her.

Earlier in the day, Shlok had sensed all was not right with me and with one look at Trisha, he started his own deductions so I had come clean. I told him about my love for her and also updated him that she had recently been betrayed by her boyfriend.

"I know that bastard Alok! She slapped him, you say. She should have kicked him in his jewels too!" Shlok had grunted after hearing the entire story.

Shlok wanted me to make my move while Naman believed I needed to give her time to heal. I agreed with Naman, I didn't want to be her temporary rebound. I wanted her for a lifetime.

Two days later, Naman walked into my office with two files in his hands.

"The accident she had, someone deliberately hit her bike and went, it was not accidental at all." He said without any formality of hellos and greetings!

"What?"

"Yes, I have not been able to track the car, because the CCTV at the junction as usual was not working that day. But I found it was a black sedan car. Some people said it looked like a black Audi, while some said black BMW. How can people confuse between Audi and BMW is beyond me!"

He plopped himself down on the seat in front of me.

"Audi or BMW? Hit her deliberately? Why would anyone want to do that? Did you find anything about her past?"

"Yes, a lot! Do you know her mother is dead?"

"Yes!"

"She died because of her dad as per the neighbours, though no complaint was ever done and it was termed as accidental death, no investigation launched either."

I frowned. Mother died because of her father. This was something only she could clarify or maybe she would never tell me anything.

"What else?"

"Her father lost his job after her mother died because he became a chronic alcoholic. He rarely comes home and neighbours say he is often found drunk on the streets or in the market near the cheap liquor shops. He has taken money from several people to buy his liquor and has quite a good debt on his head. The girls are good, homely, never cause any trouble, and in fact, are helpful in the neighbourhood but whenever he comes home, he yells, thrashes his daughters, and makes a mess!"

"Neighbours said that?"

"Yes, they all adore the two girls, there is a third sister too, married and lives in Mumbai, and comes home to visit her sisters often. But the neighbours hate their father!"

"Interesting!"

"And worrisome! The girls aren't safe if he hits them when drunk."

My head was spinning with the information Naman had offloaded in the past ten minutes and nothing made sense. There was so much going on in her life and she had always been steadfast strong and facing it all alone.

"What will you do now?"

"I don't know!"

"I think you should talk to her, make her tell you how her mother died, and if she feels unsafe, we need to make arrangements for them."

"Or we can put her father in rehab!"

"We can't, she has to agree to it, she has to give her consent!"

"Well, yeah okay!"

"Oye Romeo, don't go about doing a single thing without taking her in your confidence. You would lose the legal battle as well as your girl. What I know of her, she is strong and proud!"

I smiled at his words. How easily he had accepted her as my girl!

My girl was indeed strong and proud. And I needed to win her confidence.

"Let's find some rehab centers!"

"I can get you a list of good ones!"

I asked Trisha on our way back to her house if it was okay to take a short detour and she nodded.

"Yes, please finish up your chores, I can even go on my own."

"No, I just get a few minutes with you, don't take those away!"

"You get a full day in the office!" She laughed.

"Okay, just a few minutes outside the office!" I smiled seeing her laughing.

I parked near the Worli sea front and she frowned.

"Come!"

"Where?"

"Come!"

We sat on the stone parapet wall and she looked at the setting sun, its rays making her face glow a warm yellow. She sighed, lost in her thoughts and I watched her as she relaxed slowly watching the sun go down.

"How did your mother die?"

She stiffened next to me and tried to move back. I held her elbow and shook my head.

"I have found a few rehab centers for your father, here is the list." I gave her the sheet of paper, Naman had prepared with all the details.

"Rehab?"

"He needs treatment, Trisha, he needs to give up this habit for you girls!"

Her eyes moistened but she stayed quiet looking far at the setting sun. I thought I had lost her trust and she would choose silence like every other time. I was surprised when she softly spoke as if talking to herself.

"My mom and dad were happy together; they had built a good life. Dad worked in the factory while Mom supported him from home as much as possible. She took up small, odd jobs of stitching and sewing. She was very good with handiwork, embroidery, and stitching of clothes. I was probably in 10$^{th}$ or 11$^{th}$ grade when my dad started coming home slightly drunk. Deeksha Di was already in college and my mom frantically started looking for matches for her. They found Rajveer Jiju and she was married off as soon as she finished her college degree.

"By then my dad had started drinking more and more and came home drunk almost every night, Mom started arguing because a major part of his salary went into his latest obsession. The money was scarce I was in my final year at college, and Ana had not even started. One night Mom and Dad had a very heated argument after which he pushed her out of the house in a rage. She fell and her head hit the stairs going toward the terrace and she fell unconscious.

"He didn't let me or Ana check on her for a few hours. By the time he sobered up a little and we managed to sneak out we realized her body had turned cold. Ana and I somehow managed to rush her to the hospital. He was in his drunken state and rushed after us in panic and met with an accident on the way. He was hospitalized for a week, while Mom's dead body waited for cremation."

Tears flowed freely from her eyes and she turned to me.

"It was his fault, everyone asked us to complain and let the police take him, but how could we, Viraj? He was the only parent we had left. How could we let them take away our father too, so soon after death snatched our mother from us? Was that even an option for us girls? We told the police it was an accident and nothing more. We were all inside the house studying and resting and had not realized Mom had stepped outside."

I pulled her towards me and she buried her face in my shoulder as her body crushed into mine. She let her tears flow.

"I have never told anyone this, only Deeksha Di, and now I don't know why I am telling you all this. Please don't complain to the police, he is hurting too. He feels guilty, he knows he killed her and he drinks more trying to curb his guilt. He mourns her every day, he truly loved her and he knows he took away our mom from us, so he hurts some more."

"Then let me send him to the rehab, I will arrange for it, and he will heal. You all will be able to live your life normally, as you all deserve. Trisha, please let me do this for you?"

"Rehabs are very expensive."

"Not more expensive than your dad's life, right?"

"Why? Why are you doing this?"

"Because no matter what, I love you! I want you safe and I want you happy!"

"You? You love me?" She looked up with her doe eyes gazing into mine.

"I do, and I always will, just let me keep you safe."

"Viraj, I might be over Alok, but I don't know if I am..."

"Shhh... I am not asking you to love me back or give me anything in return. I don't want you to feel indebted either, love is not a give-and-take. I love you and that's my thing. If you love me back, I will scream with joy but if you don't I promise I will stay quiet forever, maintain my distance, and watch over you from afar! Please don't take that away from me."

She looked at me with a frown on her face, a million questions in her gaze but then she slowly nodded saying nothing at all. We sat looking out at the sea as it turned dark and then I dropped her back home. She had not just shared her family's biggest secret but she had also given me a go-ahead to find the rehab for her father.

But she had put forth a condition that she would let me pay now, and she would repay every penny over the years and I had agreed readily. If this gave her peace of mind, I was willing to take that money from her. Money meant very little to me, but it meant a lot to her because she had seen the lack of it, she had seen what money could do!

She finally smiled at me, as she got out of the car and walked inside her house. I realized I could go to the moon and come back for a smile from her. I had fallen so madly and irrevocably in love with her.

Shlok and Naman came home on a Saturday evening when I was sitting with Yuvraj playing on our Xbox.

"Hey guys!"

"Yuvi, how are you? Long time!"

"Hi Shlok Bhai, Naman dada, I am good!"

We finished off our game and the guys proposed that we go out for drinks. I refused.

"Oh, lover boy, come on, stop mopping around, all the time!" Shlok said and I looked up alarmed, Yuvi was right here.

"Lover boy? Bhai is in love!"

"Shit!"

"Bhai!"

"It's nothing, it's one-sided!"

"Who? Do I know her? I want to meet her!"

"No, Yuvi, you can't."

"Why? Why don't you ever share anything with me!" He frowned.

"Just tell him Viraj, big deal the other day she shared with you, even smiled at you right?" Shlok added and I groaned.

Why the hell had I ever mentioned anything about her in front of Shlok, he was sure to get me in trouble. Naman knew how to keep secrets but Shlok, only knew how to spill secrets, spread gossip and create trouble in everyone's life.

"Bhai, please. I will not tell a soul, I promise!"

"Trisha!"

Yuvi froze at first then frowned.

"Last time you said..."

"I lied, okay. I love her, but she doesn't."

"Yeah, she has a boyfriend!"

"Had!" Shlok added. Can't he shut his mouth? I glared at Naman who just shrugged his shoulders.

"Had?"

I put my head in both my hands. Shlok and Naman proceeded to brief my little brother about my love life, or lack of it!

The guys pulled me out to a new pub Zorro that had opened last month and I had yet to go there, this time Yuvi also joined us after all the banter at home, Yuvi and Shlok had formed a team raking their brains on how to get me my girl, while Naman and I disagreed with everything they came up with!

We were having our drinks in a corner booth, overlooking the dance floor when Naman stiffened next to me.

"Alok with his friends!" Shlok and Yuvi turned their heads to see the new group entering the nightclub.

"This guy! He never held a torch in front of you, bro, good riddance for Trisha I must say!" Shlok nudged my elbow.

"But she is still healing, he hurt her bad!"

"I can't bear to see him happy and laughing here, while she burns in pain. How mean of him, at least he should have broken things off before getting engaged to another girl!" Yuvi looked furious, ready to punch Alok for Trisha.

"I agree!" Naman said and I just nodded.

A loud laughter rang out from the group and suddenly Yuvi got up to walk towards them.

"Yuvi!" I panicked.

Shlok gestured for me to stay quiet and rushed after him. Naman held my hand, shaking his head, asking me not to move from my seat or invite everyone's attention to me.

Yuvi and Shlok returned to our booth after about 20 minutes grinning.

"We went out, bought a pack of medicines for constipation, and mixed all 10 tablets in his drink, that red drink he is sipping at right now!" Shlok updated with a stoic straight face and I looked at him in shock.

"He messes with one of ours and we mess with him. He will laugh and have fun for the next two days when he sits in the toilet nonstop!" Yuvi added.

He was annoyed because this guy had hurt his friend. He held Trisha in high regard and I was glad she had surrounded herself with some good people too. I knew, irrespective of my relationship with her, Yuvi would still be around as a friend, even if she managed to push me away.

I couldn't help but laugh with the two of them! They were grinning as if they had done the best thing ever.

"Wow! I have the craziest guys watching my back, if nothing else, you all will surely land me in jail to keep me safe!"

"Yeah, and then I will get you bailed out! If I am not inside with you." Naman added seriously and we all burst into laughter.

I had the craziest guys and I loved them so much!

I knew they would do anything for me, just as I would for them!

# CHAPTER THIRTEEN

# GETTING COMFORTABLE

***Trisha***

I couldn't believe why Viraj was always the one who got to witness the ugliest moments of my life and yet he didn't judge me, he supported me. I told Ana about our conversation about putting our dad in rehab and she agreed. I couldn't get myself to tell her that Viraj now also knew of the horror of our mother's death. We had thought of putting Dad in rehab several times, we had even researched but the costs had pushed us back, our reality still was that we couldn't afford it.

"Trish, give Viraj a fair chance, he deserves it!" Ana declared.

"Ana?"

"He loves you; can't you see? He has been always good to you, he took you that day sightseeing in Jaipur, because he knew you had never been to that city, knowing very well that you were with Alok. He brought you out safe when you created the scene at Alok's party, which by the way am so glad you did. Very unlike of you but still the best impulsive reaction if there was one. Viraj has been coaching you, helping you learn to design and be independent, he has clearly said he loves you, yet is not expecting anything in return, that is so pure. All guys just want one thing and he is not even trying."

"That's true!"

"He is searching for rehab for Dad when he doesn't need to, he just saw Dad misbehaving with you once, he understood there was a chronic drinking problem and he is finding ways to help you, help us all while keeping us safe. Think from his perspective, he has only been giving all this while, Trish, he deserves to get something too!"

I gulped, what Ana said hit something deep within me, this was what maybe I felt but never acknowledged, Viraj had been nothing but good and gentle to me, after probably the first day when he scared the shit out of me, but he had apologized and mended his ways. Ana didn't know Viraj was my stalker initially and even till a few days back when I drove back alone, he always came behind in his car.

There were some things better not shared, some little things that faded in the scheme of bigger things but still nudged me at times. He stalked quietly, never once coming close to me. The only time he came out of his car was when those roadside Romeos had cornered me. And the next day I saw the proof of what he had done to them, he had just been looking out for me, why I understood only now. He had been developing feelings for me and wanted my well-being and my safety. He was probably just getting possessive over me, which wasn't good, but no one else had cared so much for me either.

Forget stalking or showing possessiveness, no one had bothered to worry about my safety, my feelings, or my happiness so much!

I draped the silk fabric he had procured around the mannequin as per his design and stepped back to take a proper look. My back hit the wall and I froze until two hands grabbed my shoulders to steady me and his warm breath spread over my neck.

"Beautiful!" He whispered.

I relaxed immediately when I realized it was Viraj but his hold on my shoulder was firm and I didn't move. I stood with my back plastered to his front.

"When did you come?"

"When you were lost in draping the fabric, I didn't want to distract you!"

"It looks beautiful, right?"

"You? Yes!"

I frowned and looked up to find him grinning. Was he flirting with me?

"What are you looking at?" I looked up and asked him only to realize our faces were way too close, I could see the golden speckles of his dark irises. His breath hitched too at our proximity.

"You, always you!"

He nuzzled his head in my hair, taking a deep whiff, of my head. Or my shampoo? The next moment sparks flew under my pores all through my body. What was he doing to me? I gathered my thoughts, what were we talking about?

"I was asking about the dress!"

"But you are wearing jeans and a t-shirt!"

"Uff Viraj!" I stepped away and turned around to glare at him. He laughed then moved to the mannequin, frowning. Was something wrong?

"It also looks beautiful. I had not visualized this material when I did the sketch."

"Oh! What were you thinking of?"

"I was thinking of lighter fabric like a chiffon but now I see that heavier one actually suits better; the fall and pleats show up better in this!"

He touched the fabric and focussed fully on his creation.

I knocked and slowly opened the door of his cabin to find him talking on the phone with his back towards the door. He turned and smiled when his gaze met mine. He raised a finger to ask for a minute and turned back to look out of the window. I softly closed the door behind me but kept standing at it. I gazed at his muscled back clad in a white shirt, his broad well-built shoulders that could take the weight of the world, and his narrow back which tapered further into a slim waist. He was sturdy built, tall, and with not an inch of fat on his body. He must be working out regularly to maintain his physique I thought, because I had seen him eating all crap food all the time.

He always wore a bespoke suit to work, but mostly his coat hung on the back of his chair and shirt sleeves rolled up to show his muscled forearms. He cut the call and turned to focus his attention on me and I realized I had unashamedly been checking him out.

"Hey!" I walked up to his desk.

"Yes, Trisha, tell me!"

"I was wondering if I could leave a little early today?"

"What's wrong? Are you okay?" He came around his desk to stand next to me.

"Yes, yes, I am good. You know my elder sister, right, the one who is married!"

He nodded.

"She is coming home, her sister-in-law's wedding is fixed, so we were thinking we would go check out some lehengas to wear for us. Ana and I are also invited!" I smiled enthusiastically. We girls were so looking forward to the wedding.

"Oh wow, congratulations! I can design something for you girls?"

My eyes almost popped out of my sockets at his suggestion.

"Don't look at me like that, I can design, and you all can choose colours and materials. It will get stitched in far less than what you three will blow up in shops. And this will be fully customized as per your needs."

"Will it have pockets?"

He chuckled.

"Sure, can have, max 2 pockets, no more!"

"But…" I hesitated, "It will take up your time!"

"Not at all, I could reuse the designs later sometime. I would be happy to design something for you Trish, please let me!"

"Okay!" Every time he called me Trish, my heart bounced in my chest and settled back in its cavity. "You are the best!"

"Am I now?" He grinned.

Within two days he had three different yet similar-looking designs ready for all of us sisters, and in the colour shades each of us had picked. I clicked photos of the sketches and shared them with Ana and Di, to see how they found it. Within a minute, our WhatsApp group was blowing up with messages.

"Sorry, they both are hyper-excited!" I looked up at him.

He laughed and told me to take a break and chat with them. He walked over to his desk and got busy reading through some documents. I sneaked out of his room and went straight to the pantry where I made myself a cup of coffee and plopped down on one of the chairs to chat with my sisters.

They loved the designs and colours and were over the moon that he had designed these exclusively for us.

"Hello beautiful!" I looked up when someone spoke to me.

I stood up abruptly when I realized it was his cousin and his gaze was not on my face but on my chest looking down.

"Hello Sir!" What was his name? I couldn't recollect at all in this frenzy I found myself in, at his sight.

"He is Viraj and I am Sir, wow!"

I gulped, only if I could remember his name, I could call him that.

"I never see you at your desk, either you are here or in his cabin, what do you do for so long inside? Is he making you work too much?"

I shook my head. The way he said it, it was clear he was not hinting at real work, but something else altogether.

"You can come to my cabin too, once in a while and I could show you some good time too!" He brought his face close to mine and I cringed back.

What the heck!

"Hi Rohit! Long time, how are you?" Rajni thankfully walked in right then and spoke to him. He immediately took several steps back and smiled at her. She came stood next to me, talking to him, and slowly gestured for me to walk away.

"Excuse me!" I said and rushed back to my desk only to find Viraj standing there.

"Hey, I was thinking…" he froze when he looked up at me. "What's wrong?"

I shook my head, I didn't want to complain about his cousin, they were brothers after all.

"Trish, what's wrong?"

"Rohit has been making her uncomfortable!" Rajni declared and I closed my eyes.

Shit!

"Rohit? What did he do?"

"He was insinuating vile things and asking her to come to his cabin, so he could show her a good time." She clarified and Viraj frowned.

A tear fell from my eyes. I knew how mad Viraj would get hearing this and I didn't want him to know. Last time I had managed to stop him from confronting Rohit, because of a promise, but what now? I didn't want the brothers to fight because of me.

"Why are you crying, girl, it's not your fault. What he said was wrong!" Rajni wiped my lone tear. I couldn't even look up to meet Viraj's gaze but I knew he was seething in anger.

He walked away in long strides and I ran after him.

"No!" I grabbed his elbow with both my hands to stop him.

"First time, I let him be. But this I won't tolerate!" He jerked his hand out of my grasp and walked towards Rohit's cabin!

I asked Viraj what he had done to Rohit when he returned to his cabin and he gestured for me to step inside.

"He will not trouble you anymore, Trisha!"

"But… he is your brother; I never wanted any issues between you two."

"You are too good for us, and it's all fine. He crossed a line, if he had done this to anyone else as well, I would have got the HR team to reprimand him. But he insulted the one who is mine and I am not a man enough if I sit back and let it slide." He raged on.

I stood shocked at his words! I was his? Since when?

His expression sobered up as he realized what he had said in anger and he softened his next words.

"You will always be my love, my special one. You don't have to worry about a thing, Trish. He will not touch you again!"

It was Shlok's company's annual party and who's who of the business world were invited. Viraj made me come along with him and Naman. Naman was a Criminal lawyer and had nothing to do with the business fraternity but he had come because Shlok had wanted him there. Viraj and Shlok initially socialized for a few minutes with various other guests as Naman and I stood in a corner. We both barely knew anyone and had stepped aside to chat among ourselves.

I watched Viraj from a distance, working his charm with various people of all age groups. He kept bending down to touch the feet of elders while he shook hands with his contemporaries. He was so tall and probably the most handsome man in this gathering. He laughed at something an elderly gentleman said and a smile spread on my face too. He was slowly yet surely making his way in my thoughts and in my heart. I thought of him all the time, I dreamt of him every night. His simple gestures made me pause and appreciate them. His words, his smiles, I had started craving for them.

"Take a chance, Trisha, he will never hurt you like Alok did!" Naman whispered and I turned abruptly to him. I couldn't bring myself to say anything but I knew what he was trying to tell me. He was after all Viraj's friend and he was looking out for him.

Naman was a very intelligent warm and happy soul. He was caring as well because it was apparent Viraj had confided about his feelings to him. Shlok must know as well, but he didn't make a show of it or didn't go out of his way to acknowledge or care for me. Naman was suddenly like a big brother who had himself decided to adopt me.

Shlok joined us a few minutes later, but Viraj was still talking to someone on the other side of the hall.

"Trisha, you had something to drink?"

"Yeah, I did, thanks!"

"She doesn't drink alcohol; we can't take her to our wild parties!" Naman declared and I frowned.

"Can you drive a car?" Shlok asked and I nodded.

"I know driving and have a license though I only drive my *Activa* around!"

"Your *Dhanno*!" Naman chuckled and I winced.

"*Dhanno*!" Shlok laughed, "But driving *Dhanno* or *Activa* doesn't help!"

"What? Why?"

"I was thinking if you knew driving a car well, we would take you to our parties and all of us could get drunk, you could then go around dropping each one of us at our home." Shlok said with a straight face and Naman burst out laughing. I couldn't help but laugh with him.

"Okay, then I need to practice driving a car more if I want to hang around with you guys?"

"Yes! You should. In fact, take Viraj's new Merc for a spin, I am sure he won't even say no to you!" Shlok laughed.

Viraj had recently bought a Mercedes AMG GT 63, the most expensive Merc model available in India and he loved his car too much.

"He hasn't let me drive it yet!" Naman frowned.

"I know, he hasn't let me drive it either, but if she asks, he wouldn't say no!"

"Let's bet!"

Before I could tell both of them to stop, Viraj returned and put a hand around Shlok's shoulder.

"What are you guys' betting on?"

"Just that Trisha wants to drive your new Merc, and we were saying no way will you let her drive, but she insists!" Shlok twisted the tale and I looked at him surprised.

"You know how to drive a car, Trish?" Viraj looked at me and I found myself nodding. "Sure, drive us back home tonight, if you want!"

Viraj shrugged and my jaw dropped open. Naman and Shlok burst out laughing beside me. That car was worth crores of rupees.

"Told you!" Shlok grinned. And I couldn't believe Viraj had agreed to let me drive his new Merc just like that.

"Told you, take your chance!" Naman whispered in my ears and I shuddered at his words as realization hit me.

Viraj loved me far more than anything else he possessed. He had not let his best friends drive his new wheel but was willing to let me drive, because Shlok said I wanted to. I felt overwhelmed with emotions and I stepped back.

"I will just find a restroom and be back."

"That side!" Viraj pointed and I rushed away from him.

He was making me feel new sensations, new feelings. I think I was falling for him.

I stood in front of the mirror in the washroom, remembering Viraj's thoughtful gestures, little things he did for me, only for me as I felt a heat rising on my cheeks and my heart galloping hard in my chest.

"Oh, look who is here!" I turned to see two ladies enter and stand behind me.

"Do I know you?"

"We know you! You are Alok's mistress, right?"

"Alok left you so now you have hooked up with those three?"

"What nonsense!" I started to walk out as I realized one of the two ladies was Alok's fiancée.

"Running off to complain to your new boyfriends?" They laughed and I stepped out of the washroom only to freeze as I saw Alok standing right outside.

"Hello Trisha, you look good today! Is Viraj keeping you happy?" Alok grabbed both my arms and I flinched.

"Let me go!"

"Let you go, after how you humiliated me at my party? I didn't know you liked threesomes or should I say foursomes, given how you are here with three of them. They are best friends, they share everything."

I stepped back horrified at his words.

"One will woo you and once you agree, all three will share you! Have they done that already?"

"Shut up! Move away!"

"Why? You should have told me, you liked multiple men at once, I could have called my friends too."

I slapped Alok hard on his face and ran forward only to see Viraj walking towards me at some distance. I rushed towards him as he quickened his steps.

"You, okay?"

"Yes, I took care of him!"

"I was coming for you because I thought you were taking too long."

"Let's go!"

"Alok is watching us, what was he saying?"

"Nothing important, he is angry about how I humiliated him at his party."

"He deserved it!"

I turned to see Alok coming over towards us in a rage and I grabbed Viraj's hand and pulled him to a side.

"What did he say that you seem so worked up?"

"Can you kiss me?" I blurted.

"Huh? What?"

"He is watching, I want to teach him a lesson."

"Are you sure?"

I nodded as he cupped my face with both his palms.

"Anything for you!" He whispered and the next moment his lips crashed on mine.

I had asked him for this kiss yet I wasn't prepared for what would come next. He sucked on my lower lip so hard that I opened my mouth and his tongue invaded my mouth and I was a lost cause. I was lost to this world as a surge of emotions gripped my entire body setting it aflame. His hands wound around me and gently caressed my back, he pulled me close to him and I melted in his arms.

I had been kissed before but they all faded like tiny sparks in front of this raging fire he evoked in me. He devoured me and I was happy to let him. He poured all his feelings into the kiss and I realized I had fallen in love with him too. When, where, and how I didn't know, all I knew was I loved him and nothing could change that fact!

We came up for air after long and he touched his forehead to mine!

"I think I got carried away!" He whispered.

I opened my eyes to see him looking at me worriedly. He was worried that I would panic or step back but I stood my ground. I loved this man who had selflessly been there for me and slowly had become my biggest support, my biggest cheerleader.

"I did too..." I smiled and he sighed in relief. We slowly looked around to find that Alok had left but instead many others stood gaping at us. Naman made his way toward us.

"You guys could have gotten in the car or a room, instead of giving a nice show, here, right?" He spat out with his teeth gritting.

"Alok was here and we were putting on a show for him!" Viraj clarified.

"Quite some show it was!" Naman chastised us and we both giggled like school kids.

Viraj took my hand and we made our way out of the party.

"I will be known in your circles, as the one who creates a scandal and walks away in every party!" I laughed and he glared at me to shut me up. Then he shook his head and joined me, a soft laughter bubbling through him.

# GIVING UP EVERYTHING

*Viraj*

"Dad?" I barged into his bedroom late at night, when I found out what he had done earlier today.

I had been out all day today for a meeting and when I reached the office in the evening, to check my mails and see Trisha once, I found Rajni sitting alone outside my cabin in tears.

"Rajni, what's wrong?"

"Vikram Sir came today and fired Trisha!" She grabbed both my hands.

"What?" I was baffled by her actions as well as her words. I looked around, and yes Trisha's desk was empty.

"Yeah, not just fired, he humiliated her very badly that too shouting on the top of his voice making at least two floors hear all the commotion."

Rage flooded my veins.

"What did he say?"

"He said she was..." She sobbed, looking uncomfortable to continue but I nodded and urged her to go on, I needed to know, what he accused her of. "She was sleeping with you, to further her career. That she was a slum dweller with dreams higher than she should ever have. That she didn't deserve this job, she was just a... just a slut and should go try her luck in the red-light area. He also shouted that she was trying to manipulate you and get you to fall for her charms."

I was angry beyond reason. He had no right to say any of this to her. She was poor yes, but she had never done a wrong by him or anyone else for that matter.

"Dad?" I came to stand in front of him.

"Viraj, come. I was waiting for you. So, you met your little mistress?"

"She is not my mistress, and you had no right to speak to her like that!" I raged on.

"Viraj, is this how you talk to your dad?" My mom chastised me.

"Do you have any idea what he called that naïve girl, he called her a slut and what not that too in office! I gave her a job, who are you to fire her?"

"I am still the owner with rights, I can even fire you!"

"Really, then fire me!"

"For her? Viraj, those kinds of girls are okay to sleep with, not to bring them to office or home!"

"Dad!" I roared. I was furious and was having a tough time controlling myself from punching him at the moment.

By now rest of the family had also gathered behind me. Yuvi stepped closer to me when he realized who were we arguing about.

"She even tried to make a pass at Rohit, but he was smart enough to dodge her attempts and then she went and framed him for talking trash."

"Trisha would never do that!" Yuvi screamed and I winced.

"You too? Has she worked her charms on both my sons?"

"Enough dad. She has done nothing of the sort! She is just doing her job and that too a good one at it. Hire her back and apologize to her!"

"I won't! Never ever will I apologize to that piece of worthless shit!"

"Then I won't work in your company either!"

"Viraj!" My mom gasped.

"Fine, you too can get lost! Go behind that girl and screw up your life. But before that get out of my house too."

"Vikram, no!"

"You are right dad, I don't want to live in your house, or work in your company if this is how you treat everyone, if this is what you think of every young poor girl, that she is making her career advance by sleeping around, of course you would know, you helped several such girls in your lifetime. But Trisha is better than them, and I am not you!" I smirked.

"Get out!" He roared.

"Happy to!" I stormed out of his room and went straight to my room with Yuvi and Vandana at my heels.

"Bhaiya!" Vandana hugged me, her eyes filled with unshed tears.

"It's okay. I am just leaving this house, not you guys, okay? But I cannot work for him if this is the attitude he has."

"I am with you, Bhai! I will also come!"

"No! You stay out of this matter, Yuvi. You are studying, your exams are starting next week, you will not hamper your studies or anything. I will be fine; I can work and earn. I will stay in touch with you!"

"But Bhai, how can he say such things for Trisha?"

"His words reflect on his character, not hers!"

"Right!"

"Where will you go, bhaiya?" Vandana asked.

"I will figure something out!" I patted her head.

I packed a bag with some of my essentials, my clothes, and my sketchbooks and walked out of the house. As I picked up the car keys to step out, I heard my dad's voice behind me.

"Leave that car behind, it's purchased from Rajvansh Industries money!"

I turned on my heels and threw the keys back at him. My mom tried to stop me, saying I must apologize to my dad but I refused to. Apologizing to him was out of the question, he was the one who needed to apologize to Trisha.

Kaki Ma and Vikash Kaka were not happy with this but they stayed quiet, just pleading with me to not cut everyone out of my life. I never intended to.

I stepped out of the house, got a cab, and called Naman.

"Bro, what is the name of the building where you live?"

"My apartment? You don't know the name?"

"Dude, are you there?"

"Yes! What's wrong?"

"I am coming over, give me the name of the building, I need to tell the cab driver, I know the way, not the name."

Naman laughed out loud then gave me the building name and cut the call.

"What's wrong? Where are you going?" He asked as he saw the two bags in my hand.

"Bro, can I stay here with you for a couple of days? Just a few days till I can figure something out."

"Of course, come on in."

I told Naman everything that had happened.

"He didn't let you bring your car. But you bought it. That's mean!"

"No! I got my sketchbooks, and my laptop and..." I froze mid-sentence.

All my hard work was on the office laptop and sketches in the office. Naman understood and stood still too.

"Office?" He asked. I loved that about him, he understood the unspoken words, the innermost thoughts, and fears.

"Yes!"

"Let's get it out now before he gets his hands on them."

"Let's call Shlok, we have a lot of things!" I mumbled.

We ran out of his house and Naman drove his SUV like a maniac while I called Shlok and put the phone on speaker.

"Hi Shlok, drop everything you are doing and come to my office."

"Dude, I am in the middle of... Not coming now."

"There is no choice given, it's an emergency, of the highest grade, drop everything and come."

"Shlok, come fast and get your biggest car, if possible, your Kushaq." Naman yelled.

"Naman, Viraj! Damn it you, guys!" We heard some shuffle and background noises, then the call got dropped.

He called back two minutes later and started screaming.

"I was inside her, couldn't you both have waited for like 1 more minute?"

"We didn't know, dude, that you get done in a minute!" I chuckled.

"Next time we will call you after that one minute, I promise!" Naman added and we both guffawed. Shlok gruntled but stayed quiet.

All three of us reached my office almost at the same time and rushed upstairs. I asked Naman to gather everything from Trisha's desk while I pulled Shlok inside my cabin.

"Every single thing!"

"Yes, lover boy!"

"Will you tell me what's going on?" Shlok stopped at the door absolutely confused. He thought we were here to prank someone or raid the liquor bottles in my dad's cabin.

"Yes, come inside, pack up everything while I tell you, we don't have time."

I narrated everything to Shlok, while we packed up my stuff from my cabin, my laptop, my pen drives, all design sketches, and the material I had procured on my own for my new collection. The designs Trisha had helped me create. We wiped clean, every single thing.

I was glad I had not discussed my plan of launching a new brand outside of Rajvansh Group yet with my dad, I had been thinking of discussing it this week.

"Let's go!" I declared when I thought I had gathered everything I wanted to take and everything I would need.

"Wait!" Shlok paused.

"What?"

"So many bottles here, we can't leave them behind, they will feel abandoned.!" Shlok smirked.

"Seriously?" Naman asked while I just shook my head.

Shlok packed up all the good whiskey and scotch bottles too.

We stuffed both of their cars with all the stuff we had got, leaving a very confused security guard behind, and headed back to Naman's house, where I would need to camp out for a while. I had enough money in my bank account to be able to buy a place quickly and move out of there. Till then I knew Naman would be happy to let me live with him. Even Shlok had asked me to come over and stay with his family. But I refused, Shlok's dad was a good friend of my dad too.

Shlok's mom was an angel but somehow Shlok never got along with her, I knew there were issues in his family and the dynamics were even worse than my own family. At least I didn't hate my mom like Shlok hated his mom. Naman was good, just a father-son duo and they both got along beautifully. Naman's dad got along with us too better than our own dads.

The next morning, I woke up to the shock that my father had blocked all my cards and even the bank account I had of my own. I was now truly homeless and penniless. I told Naman and he was furious.

"I can file a case, he can't do this, not your personal bank account at least!"

"I can't believe he would do this, what will the case do? It will take forever to unfreeze the accounts!"

"Let it, but I am filing that case anyway, let me see how to expedite it. What now?"

"I will open a new account, I was in talks with a French brand to launch my designs in collaboration with them, my dad has no idea about this, I think I should expedite that and launch it sooner."

"Good idea, you have everything you need to start the talk with them?"

"Yes, our stash from last night, this is what I had rushed to gather!"

"You should talk to Trisha too!"

"Yes, that's what I was thinking, I will get ready, apologize to her on my dad's behalf and ask her to work with me on this collection, she had been working on it from day one anyway."

"I will come with you!"

"No, don't pause your life for me, I can go."

"I have the day off today, no case and nothing urgent either. I will come along."

I knocked on her door, to find Ana at home.

"She has been crying since she returned yesterday!" She whispered seeing me and Naman at the door.

"Trish, come Viraj Bhaiya has come to see you!" She called out and Trisha came out looking devastated.

"Trisha!" I rushed forward to her.

"Viraj, please go, I can't take any more humiliation!"

"Do you think I will ever humiliate you? I came to apologize for what happened yesterday, I only got to know in the evening."

"In front of the entire office, what was my fault? Because I kissed you? I am so sorry!"

"Trisha, it wasn't your fault!"

"But it was, I forgot for a moment that you belonged to the upper class, the top cream, and I was not allowed to dream or aspire for anything big in my life. But Viraj, I never once intended to use that kiss for any gains, I was only doing my work, and trying to earn my living. I am sorry for asking you to kiss me in that impulsive moment. But this was not the punishment I deserved."

I cupped her face; she wasn't giving me a chance to say anything. She was hurt, she was humiliated.

"I don't have the riches, the money to throw around, all I have is my honour and zeal to work hard and he snatched both away yesterday. I don't think I can even face you now, please go!"

"Trisha, I left everything, him, the house, the company!"

"Why?"

"If he cannot respect you, I cannot respect him. If he won't let you work in Rajvansh Group, I won't work there either."

She looked at me horrified.

"No! Don't do that. Don't fight with your dad for me. I am a nobody; he is your father. Rajvansh group is your legacy, your dream. No, no, go back and apologize or whatever but make up with your father.!" She tried to push me away from her.

"You are not a nobody, Trisha!" I yelled.

"Viraj, please go back before I lose the last shred of honour I have at least here in the neighbourhood!"

"I love you, Trisha!"

"No, don't. This is not love, you are just infatuated with me! You can't love me; it will only ruin your life!"

"You don't love me, and that I can accept. But you have no right to tell me, what I can do or cannot! Whether I ruin my life or make it, it will be for you! All these months, and you still have no clue about how much I love you? How dare you call it infatuation?"

I turned around and walked out of her house. She was not even ready to listen to me, I agreed that she was hurt but how could she tell me what I felt for her would fade away? I gestured for Naman to come but he stood rooted in his spot, his face mirroring my anger and hurt.

# CHAPTER FIFTEEN

# REALIZATION HITS HARD

## *Trisha*

I felt so wrecked within by the way I was thrown out of his company and humiliated that I didn't want to face anyone. I knew he would come, my heart even waited for him last night, but he didn't come. That added to my misery and today when he came, I wanted him to take me in his arms and take my pain away, like he always did but then he said that he had left his house, his company everything for me. My heart soared in joy but the next moment I crashed back on earth as I realized what a big responsibility it was on me, and I was done with bearing responsibilities and expectations of others. I didn't want this!

I loved him with all my heart and I couldn't see him looking so desolate, he was used to the spoilt rich life, all his grown-up years, all he had dreamt of - was to be the CEO of the Rajvansh group of industries and if he gave it up for me, he would always somewhere deep in his heart resent me for it. I couldn't let him give up on his biggest dream.

I didn't want to bear the responsibility of him separating from his family, him living the life of a common person, without the riches; the struggles, the little sacrifices I was so used to making. I didn't want to bear the responsibility of seeing his dreams shatter right in front of his eyes. I knew he would never utter a word or accuse me of it, but I didn't want even the thought to cross his mind, later in life, that if not for Trisha, maybe I would have had everything I wanted. I couldn't shoulder that burden, that pain, that resentment that would come along with this decision of his.

So, in my panic, I asked him to leave and go back. He was so furious when I broke his heart saying that he didn't love me. He stormed out of the house and I was about to collapse down and cry. I had truly lost everything today but then Naman grabbed both my shoulders and shook me hard. The one I thought loved me as an elder brother loved him far more and it was evident. His words cut across my heart but I knew he was right to be angry at me for hurting his friend.

"How dare you? How dare you tell him it is infatuation and not love?"

"Naman!" I whimpered.

"He has been crazy for you for past year, he was a Casanova, who slept with random girls every night and since the day he laid his eyes on you, a year back, he has not slept with one girl, not one. Since the day he got drunk and you scrunched your nose because of the liquor smell, he hasn't touched his drinks even once. He gave up his easy life, his company, his house, his family all for you and you say he doesn't love you?

"Last night we went to his office to steal all of his hard work, your hard work, the designs, the laptops, the materials he had bought so you could work with him and you don't have to start from scratch. His dad kicked him out of the house, he had no car, and all his accounts and cards were blocked. He is penniless, all because he stood for you, for his love. He is living in my home unsure when he will be able to move out, I am his best friend and I love him enough to let him stay forever but imagine the blow to a self-made man's ego, becoming homeless, penniless overnight just because he chose love over everything else. He fought with his father for you, Trisha!

"If you can't love him back, fine, he can live. He has been living all these months, loving you caring for you, knowing you may never reciprocate his feelings but you have no right to ask him to go back to his father or to apologize. You have no right to tell him, it's not love, its infatuation! Do you even know what infatuation is? What love is? If you can't mend his heart and support him, you have no right to break his heart, clip his wings and shatter him completely."

"Naman!"

He huffed and walked out in a rage. He was angrier than Viraj on his behalf and I slumped down finally breaking apart. Ana tried to hold me together, but when she couldn't manage, she freaked out and called Deeksha Di.

"I love him Di..."

I howled out as Ana and Di hugged me tight after Ana quickly narrated to Di that Viraj had confessed his love to me, left his home, his company everything for me and had come here in the morning to apologize because his dad kicked me out of the company yesterday.

"Trish, then why did you send him away like that?" Ana implored.

"I couldn't ruin his life. He was taking this impulsive decision, he was taking this stand but he has grown up in luxury, within a few days he will resent all this and then he will resent me cause all this would then be my responsibility. Today, Naman said he gave up on everything for me, tomorrow Viraj would think the same that he had to give up on all riches because of me!"

"Oh, Trish!" Di spoke understanding my rationale.

"You are hurting, there he is hurting. It's not right!" Ana said.

"Viraj is angry, even Naman is!"

"Who is Naman now?" Di looked up confused.

"Viraj bhaiya's friend, who brought him here, where bhaiya is staying now."

"He is angry because Viraj is staying with him, because of you?"

"No... no... he was angry on behalf of bhaiya!" Ana went on to explain to Di everything slowly including the words of Naman too this time.

"He sounds like a true friend!" Di sighed.

"That he is, and I love him so much for that!" I acknowledged.

"You love Naman?"

"Oh God! I love Viraj, what do I do?" I groaned and Ana giggled.

We both glared at her and she schooled her expressions.

"What do you want? You must tell Viraj that you love him and still don't want him to give up everything!"

"Then he will think I love him for his money!"

"True!"

"I can call Yuvi here; you can tell him your rationale and he can talk to Bhaiya?"

"No!" I looked up horrified.

"No! That won't be right!" Di spoke thoughtfully. Di was thinking this through, she rarely ever was impulsive.

"Trish, I think you should talk to Viraj. You both need to communicate, he needs to know you love him, tell him to make up with his dad even if he doesn't work with him. You must support him, he has only been good to you, Trish, all these months. He knew you loved Alok and yet he was good to you!"

"Yes Trish, I agree with Di, bhaiya needs to know he is loved, that he is not alone. We all are his family!" Ana said and I realized he must be so lonely right now.

I stood up.

"I will go to meet him!"

"Now?"

"Yes!"

"Like this, in your shorts?"

"Oh!" I looked down at myself and then ran inside to take a shower and get dressed.

I got ready and dialled his number. He picked up my call in one ring.

"Hello, Viraj!"

"Yes!"

"I need... Viraj... I..." My voice started choking up.

"What's wrong? Where are you?" His voice was panicked.

My heart broke all over again, how could I hurt him, how could I think for a minute that he would resent me? I broke his heart and sent him away, and yet he picked up my phone on the first ring and was now panicking because I was sobbing on the phone.

"Where are you?"

"Huh?"

"I need your address; I need to talk to you!"

"Why?"

I wanted to tell him that I loved him but no, that was something I could only say to him face to face. I needed him to give me his address.

"Naman said you got my things also from the office last night?"

"Oh, right! I will send you the address right away." His voice was pained and sounded distant.

He opened the door and I launched myself at him. He looked so desolate, so tired. I hugged him tight putting my arms around his neck. He stood frozen.

"I love you, Viraj!"

"Huh?"

"I love you so much!" I looked at his face and saw surprise flicker in his gaze. He slowly pulled me inside and shut the door of the apartment but kept standing in the entryway.

"But... you?" He finally spoke.

"I love you; I didn't want to hurt you. I didn't want you to fight with your dad for me, I didn't want you to resent me in the future that because of me, you had to give up on your lavish life, on your dreams, on your company. I will never be able to bear the responsibility of your grief, of your shattered dreams, Viraj!" I said it all out in one breath, I didn't want this to weigh me down anymore.

"Oh, Trisha! I would never. How can I ever resent you? You are the best thing that ever happened in my life. Yes, I had a lavish lifestyle but that didn't define me, neither was I used to it. I do not get along with my parents either, so there is no love lost. If not now, sometime in the future I would have surely branched out, guess I knew I would that is why I was working on this new collaboration on my own."

"Oh!"

"Come here, so what were you saying, that you love me?"

I nodded as I stepped closer to him.

"For real?"

I nodded again as I smiled feeling too shy now that we were face to face.

"I need to hear the words, Trish!"

"I love you, Viraj, love you so much!" I whispered.

"You make me the happiest man on Earth, Trish! I love you so much!" He pulled me in a bone-crushing hug and swirled me around.

"What the heck?" Naman's voice made us jump apart. "You guys made up as well."

"She loves me!" He grinned back at Naman with a childlike glee.

Naman stood shocked, looking at me, then at him, then shook his head.

"And here I was worrying for you both unnecessarily!" He sighed dramatically and walked inside his room.

"Come!" Viraj took my hand in his and walked towards a room with purpose. "I need to kiss you without interruptions!" He declared before shutting the door and pulling me in a hug. His lips sought mine and I melted at the way they cajoled mine to open up for him. Something ignited deep within my core, a fire of passion, of desire, making me wish to give everything to him, wanting me to surrender to him and comforting me that he wouldn't hurt me ever.

"Viraj!" I whispered as we came up for air and he touched his forehead to mine.

"Sorry, I couldn't contain my happiness. I love you and we will go as slow as you want."

How could one not fall for this man?

I couldn't believe he was the same man who had stalked me for days on end, not saying a word, and how scared I had felt on the first day of work that I had contemplated resigning from my job.

"I trust you and I love you more than everything in my world but is it right to give up everything, your company, your family?" I raised my concern one more time.

He kissed my forehead softly breathing in deeply.

"You are my family, Trish, the company I will start now, with you will be mine. My dad and I always had a lot of issues, I guess we were just waiting for one spark to explode, and this incident provided that to us. We are both very strong-headed men, if not now, I surely would have parted ways from him, sometime down the line, because I love my independence way too much."

I understood where he was coming from and I was here to support him in whatever decision he took. I pulled him in a hug and he picked me up in his arms.

"You gave up drinking? Why?" I remembered and moved my face back from where I had it buried in his neck to look at him.

"Yes, I did. Because you didn't like the smell of it, and later when I learned your mom's story, I realized why you were so scared that day in my cabin when you saw the liquor bottle on my desk. I wasn't drunk that day, I was jealous, mad with rage that Yuvi got your smiles while I didn't."

"So, you won't drink ever again?"

"Nope, I won't drink ever again, because I know it makes you uncomfortable, it makes you remember things that you want to forget!"

"Oh, Viraj!" I moved my face to kiss him but he pulled back.

"How did you get to know?"

"Naman mentioned when he scolded me, today?"

"Naman scolded you?" He slid me down and let me stand. "When?"

"When you walked out of my house, he came like the most protective best friend and scolded me for breaking your heart and saying those hurtful things. I understand his point of view, I was just trying to shield you from long-term heartbreak not thinking of the present."

"He is a gem; Shlok is as well and they both couldn't be more different than each other. I am so lucky to have them watching my back, as I would watch theirs whenever the need arises."

I smiled, yeah that's what friends were for and I had no friends at all. I had lost all my friends when I grew up overnight and had to take on all the responsibilities.

"You wait and watch how they will adore you too!" He chuckled and I knew his friends were going to love me just as much as they loved him.

By evening all the news channels reported that Viraj had stepped down from the CEO position of Rajvansh Group of Industries over some ideological differences and Rohit Rajvansh was taking up the CEO role alongside the CFO role.

"Rohit? Really?" Naman asked Viraj who just shrugged. All three of us were in his living room in front of the TV.

"Rohit has always been trying too hard to stay in my dad's good books, guess it's his reward time."

"I would have thought your dad would take the reins; this makes everything more permanent!"

"Exactly my point, he is trying to convey that it is permanent and he is not leaving the option of me returning open with this announcement, not that I am keen on."

"Are you sure?"

"Yes, I am sure and this also means that I am now free to announce my entity and my own design brand."

"I know a few lawyers, will get the paperwork started, leave it with me, you just think of an apt name."

Viraj turned to me and I shrugged, what did I know about the brand names and such?

We had to delay my dad's admission into the rehab center Viraj had finalized because of the sudden money crunch he found himself in. We both worked long hours to ensure that our collection was ready, the deal with the French Brand had come through and they were willing to launch the new collection as early as next month if we were ready with the collection and all the paperwork that was needed to launch Viraj's new company.

Naman had suggested that instead of launching just a brand or working as an individual, Viraj should first launch his design firm and then associate that with the French Brand, it would give more credibility, and hiring more people or getting finances would then become easier.

For all fabric and other embellishment procurement, we both had to run around and my *Activa* came in very handy. He was so tall that sitting behind me while I drove was a major challenge for him. His feet touched mine at the front. But he was learning to make do with whatever he had, whatever was available. He hated it that he had no choice but to depend on me, Naman, and Shlok for basics. But he was also taking it all in good spirits, not once had he shied away from travelling not in his fancy cars or lifting the material himself to get it back home.

Viraj found a part-time teaching faculty job in a design institute and took weekend classes. This brought in some money and freed up all week for him, where he focussed on his new company, designing, and working on the launch. I pleaded with the pharmacy shop I used to work at to let me work part-time again, but they had found someone for the evening in the months that I had left, so they asked me to manage the shop over the weekends. This worked out even better for me because I could spend long hours all week with Viraj and on weekends, we both worked long hours to earn.

I had just finished adding the final touches to the design we were working on, when I felt Viraj's hand go around my waist from behind. I wore a black palazzo pant and a light blue linen top today and his arms brushed the skin of my midriff. I looked at him from the corner of my eyes and he put his forehead on my shoulder.

"I am so tired, Trish!"

"Do you want to take a nap? I will step out and sketch while you rest a little. You haven't slept last night."

"Not that, I am just too tired, Trish, I don't know, like exhausted."

I turned around slowly and kissed him. He deepened the kiss but it was gentle today, not the scorching hot kiss where he showed me how much he craved me. This kiss was caressing my soul, demanding me to shelter him and provide him with what his heart desired.

"Can you sit with me for a while?"

The strain of the last few days was showing on his face now. He had been working too hard, sleeping barely 3-4 hours each night, because he wanted to launch the company and our collection at the earliest. Weekends were busy too.

I sat on the bed, with my back rested against the headboard and beckoned him to come over. He laid down with his head in my lap, his fingers playing with my hair. He pushed my top up a little bit and softly kissed the skin of my tummy making me shudder. He then pulled the top back in place and nuzzled his face in. My heart melted at his gesture and I sat undecided whether I was ecstatic with what he just did or whether I was sad that he stopped at just one kiss.

I ran my fingers over his forehead and his hair softly. He breathed me in sharply and lay still, while I sat with my fingers drawing circles on his head, trying to soothe him. Soon, his breath became even and he fell into a deep sleep and I put my head against the headboard to close my eyes too.

We were working out of Naman's house only and we had gotten close now that we were in a relaxed setting. We were partners now, not a boss and employee. In his new company, he made sure that we both were 50-50 partners in the company that he named – *Virsha*.

Virsha – Viraj & Trisha Creations

I couldn't believe it when Naman gave me some papers and said he needed my signatures. I kept looking at him puzzled but he only smiled and said it was Viraj's decision.

"It's our collection, our creation, and our first baby, Trish! Of course, we are equal partners in this, in life, and in everything!"

My breath hitched at his words, our first baby! Equal partners in life?

"You will marry me, right, I have nothing much to offer, no money, no big name, no stability but I will work hard. I will work 25 hours of the 24 I have to make it all good for you, to make spending your life with me worth it, I promise!"

I hugged him tight nodding. I loved him so much and I could see his dedication and hard work in everything. I had never had anything much to start with, but to have everything, every luxury, and giving it all up to start from scratch was not easy at all but not once had he shown his disappointment or frustration. He kept moving on, keeping his head high.

"You moron!" Naman grunted and we both broke apart.

"What?" Viraj looked at both his friends, who stood glaring at him.

"Is this the way to propose to a girl?" Shlok called him out and he looked at me sheepishly.

I blushed at the realization that they were the witness to this confession and that yes, in a way Viraj had proposed to me for marriage and I had already accepted. I buried my face in his chest and all three of them burst out laughing.

"Trisha, don't let him off so easily!" Naman added and I laughed.

"Bro!" Viraj protested.

# CHAPTER SIXTEEN

# FALLING FOR HIM

## *Trisha*

Viraj and I were working together locked in our room at Naman's house, it had started feeling like our room, given the amount of time we were spending here, we were giving the final touches for the collection launch next weekend, when I felt Viraj's hand circle my waist and I leaned back on him, resting my head on his chest. He often held me like this and I found comfort in him.

He brushed his nose behind my right ear and I was a goner, his hot breath spread through my neck and I sighed. He kissed the pulse point on my throat, holding me tight, my back plastered to his front and I involuntarily moaned only to make him grunt and I felt his desire for me growing hard and poking me at the back.

His right hand snaked up and lightly brushed my left breast and I sucked in a sharp breath. Viraj had only kissed me and hugged me, he had never taken any liberties, neither had he ever touched me how he touched me now.

"Do I stop?" He asked brushing his thumb over my pebbled nip and a moan escaped me.

Even though there were two layers of clothing in between, still his thumb had managed to make me want him to touch me more.

"Trish?"

"No! Don't stop!" I whispered.

He turned me around as he crashed his lips on mine and I was transported to heaven. He knew how to kiss a girl thoroughly. And he always knew when to be gentle and caring and when to be crushing scorching hot and unforgiving. Right now, he was pouring his passion into me through his mouth, oh damn this man, was making me ache for something that I didn't know existed.

I pushed my body closer to him if that was even possible and he started moving back toward the bed. I moved with him until we both crashed on the bed, me lying on top of him. I tried to move but he groaned and I realized his length was hard and so big. It felt much bigger and I worried that it would hurt me even more.

He flipped us on the bed in a swift move and crashed his lips back on mine, stealing all the thoughts away and making me want to surrender completely and be with him just like this all my life. He trailed his lips down my chin, nibbling on my chin, dropping featherlight kisses all over my neck, licking it, and blowing air on it. I was in heaven, if his touch, his soft kisses felt so good, I never wanted to come back to earth.

He pulled my t-shirt down one shoulder and proceeded to nibble on my skin there. I could feel his hard length poking me on my tummy and he was not even trying to hide it, I understood what was coming next. Alok never even waited to kiss me so thoroughly like how Viraj was cherishing each inch of my body, going painstakingly slow as if he was relishing the feel and taste of my skin as he exposed it inch by inch kissing it lavishly.

"I am not a virgin!" I blurted and his head shot up, his eyes dazed.

"Neither am I." He replied and went back to the task at hand of kissing my shoulder blades.

Why was he going so slow, maybe he thought it was our first time, so he wanted to give me space or maybe he wanted me to do something too. I remembered once Alok had yelled at me for not participating and laying on the bed like a dead body. I impulsively moved my hands to remove my t-shirt and Viraj looked up frowning.

"Sweetheart?" He sat up and looked at me, "What are you doing?"

"Removing... I mean how do you want?"

"Want what?" He frowned as his gaze peered into mine.

Nervousness engulfed me and I had never found myself so tongue-tied, so conscious. Why was he talking and asking questions? Shouldn't he be taking control and telling me what to do? He adjusted his length but kept sitting and watching me.

"Do you want to go all the way?" He finally asked.

"I thought you wanted to!"

"Why are you sounding so scared? I won't do a thing that you don't want and frankly I never thought of doing anything at all today, I just impulsively..." He paused, "Why are you scared?" He frowned again and I realized I was shivering.

"I am scared!" I blurted.

"Come here, are you still scared of me? I won't hurt you!"

I shook my head.

"Then?"

"You are bigger, it will hurt!"

He chuckled.

"What a boost to my ego, but you are experienced too, and no it won't hurt, it will just make you feel even better!"

I sat there looking at him confused.

"But it always hurt!" The words I had never wanted to utter in front of anyone escaped me.

He frowned and pulled me up in a hug.

"It is not supposed to hurt, did he not make you feel good before pushing in?" I just kept looking at him and he kissed my forehead softly.

"Trish sweetheart, I am not doing a thing today, even though this wasn't planned, relax, don't be scared of me. And when I make love to you, I promise it won't hurt at all, it will only feel good, oh so good!"

He pulled me in a hug and nuzzled his head in my hair, I buried my face in his chest soaking myself in his warmth and his unique scent. He stopped the moment he felt I was uncomfortable. Alok had given me to understand that men couldn't stop once they started and it was all his selfish nature to take more and more from me. Probably he was with me only for this, after all, he had his childhood sweetheart and his fiancée already waiting for him on the side.

I shook my head and chastised myself for thinking of my past and Alok when I felt so good in Viraj's arms. I never thought I would feel this peace and feel so loved ever in my life. He came like my guardian angel and was making my life so worth living.

"I love you!" I whispered.

"I love you more!" He whispered back and I realized that was quite possible, he had so completely devoted himself to me and my life. He gave up everything he had, his family, his work, his entire life of all these years for me. Would I have been able to do the same if the roles were reversed? I wasn't sure.

Yuvi opened the door, when I rang the bell the next morning at Naman's house and I looked at him surprised. Naman had gone to stay with his dad for a few days, Viraj mentioned he alternated quite often.

"Trisha, how are you?"

"I am good, how are you?" I was seeing Yuvi after a long while.

"I am good, just came to meet bhai. Thank you!"

"Thank you for?" I looked at him puzzled.

"For standing by him, for taking care of him, while we all abandoned him. I am so glad; he has finally found you and with you, he will find his family!"

I frowned and looked back, but Viraj was not to be seen anywhere.

"Family?"

"Bhai would never say but after him, my mom had a daughter who died within a few days and my mom slipped into depression. My dad is not a very emotional person and they both completely ignored him; he must have been 3 or 4 years old at the time and he was suddenly left without his parents until my uncle and aunt took it upon themselves to care for him. After a few years, I was born and mom bounced back to life and cared for the new baby, forgetting yet again that she had an older son, who also craved her attention.

"He never got the love and affection of a mother that he deserved, and the distance between him and our parents has always been huge, I tried to fill it when I grew up and started understanding things, and so did Kaki Ma but something has always been missing and today I see content and happiness in his eyes. By giving up on all of us and finding you, he has finally found his happiness."

My heart broke for Viraj, he never uttered a word about this and he would never have in the future too. I was glad Yuvi told me because now I could make it my purpose in life to shower him with abundant love and care.

"Thanks, Yuvi for sharing this with me!"

"He would never say it!" Yuvi paused and I nodded, "But I think you as his partner need to know, what he lacks and what he craves! Being someone's center of the world!"

"Don't we all crave it?"

"We do!" He smiled and for the first time in all these years, I noticed the similarity between the two brothers.

Our conversation had moved to Yuvi's plans of master's and the exams that were going on for them, when Viraj stepped out fresh from shower looking like a Greek God, dressed in a blue denim shorts and black t-shirt. He paused in the hallway looking at us then moved to Kitchen without disturbing us.

Yuvi saw he was back and took my leave, going in the kitchen to talk to Viraj. I stopped at the door of the kitchen.

"Bhai, take care, and let me know if you need anything."

"Thanks, Yuvi, you take care and message me often bro, I miss you!"

"Oh Bhai, I miss you so much!" Yuvi hid his face in Viraj's neck and I realized these brothers were as close as we sisters were.

Viraj made breakfast for both of us, while I prepped for our lunch after Yuvi left.

"All your wedding lehengas are ready, do you want to try them on?"

"Wow! Yes! Here?"

"Yes, Yuvi got me my camera, it's a super expensive one that I bought in the US when I was studying there. You know my dad sold off my Merc, so before he raided my room, Yuvi sneaked things out, that he thought were special to me and brought some today, along with a bag of clothes and has promised to bring them to me, slowly whenever dad isn't around."

I stood speechless, even if they had a tiff, how could his dad sell off his car? He loved his car. My dad was no good, drank and yelled at us all day but at least never intentionally hurt us. He never sold off any of Mom's jewellery or any of the household things to pay off his debt. I shuddered at the thought. He hadn't returned home in the past two days and I seriously hoped he was okay. I would try and search for him in the evening but work for now.

I wore the blush pink lehenga that I had made for myself first and opened the door of the room for Viraj. He turned and his eyes grew darker as his breath hitched.

"Mesmerising! You look divine, Trish!"

"Can you help with the hooks at the back?" I whispered and he nodded turning me around, then grunted loudly.

"Damn, you are leaving your hair open at the wedding!"

I laughed at his possessiveness. The blouse was almost backless with just two buttons at the bottom and a tying thread at the top. He trailed the tips of his fingers over my bare back and I moaned. He leaned down to bite my back and I shuddered; he kissed the spot immediately after making me go weak in my knees. He straightened, pulled me in a hug as his hands went around my waist, dropping a soft kiss on my shoulder.

"I am going to remove this lehenga from your body, one day!" He whispered in my ears and I shuddered at the dark promise in his voice. I realized I wanted that too. The way he had reacted seeing me in this lehenga, I wanted to see how he would react when it came off.

He took me to another room, where he had set up his camera and asked me to pose in the Lehenga. I was very conscious and he promised that the images would be used for advertisements of our brand but in all the pictures he clicked, my face didn't show properly. I either looked at the other side, or my hair or my hand covered most of my face.

We continued clicking photos with all three lehengas, my blush pink, Di's mesmerizing grey lehenga, and Ana's fiery orange one. I knew the colours would suit them both and we three were going to look oh so beautiful. Di had also got a designer saree made for herself for the Sangeet function, but Ana and I had decided to skip that function altogether.

"When is the wedding?"

"This Sunday!"

"And what about the Sangeet, what are you wearing for it?"

"Ana and I aren't going for Sangeet, it's on Friday, and with Ana's exams going, she can't go. I didn't want her to feel left behind, so I explained to Di and she understood as well. The main wedding is enough for us."

He nodded slowly.

"Why don't you try on the saree too, am sure Deeksha won't mind!"

"Oh, she wouldn't mind at all, she is a giver, almost a second mother to us."

I wore the maroon sequined saree for the photoshoot and after we were done, Viraj started removing it and I froze.

"Not this, please!"

He stepped back immediately.

"This isn't mine; I want to make memories with what is mine!"

He chuckled.

"Then you didn't let me remove the pink lehenga!" He whined and I laughed. "You trust me, right?"

I nodded.

I trusted him more than I trusted myself!

I had somehow convinced Viraj to come with me in the Mumbai Local train for the day, we wanted to cover multiple places to check out the fabrics and place orders locally. I was in no mood to drive in Mumbai's crazy traffic with a crazy Viraj behind me. He was so tall that whenever I had to stop the bike, he just jammed his feet on the road making me lose balance.

"It's so crowded!" He frowned and I had to pull him inside the train, or else he would have just kept standing on the platform.

"Shhh, this isn't... we are in first class!"

"Then what happens in second class?"

"You would have been touched and felt by so many ladies by now!" I laughed and he looked at me horrified.

"Seriously?"

"Well, we girls face it every time, so I am guessing a tall handsome guy might also get mauled." Someone bumped into me and he immediately changed his stance to cover my body with his, shielding me completely.

"You are not travelling in local trains!"

"But it is the same in the buses as well, on the crowded streets!"

He grunted in frustration.

"Damn it, the first thing I am buying when I save up is a car!"

"For me?" I teased him.

"For you, everything for you sweetheart!" He replied earnestly.

I knew he had grown up in luxury but I enjoyed this too. Travelling in Mumbai's locals, in the crowded buses also had a charm of its own, though it was stressful at times, but it was a quick and easy way to commute too.

I brought lunch that I had made at home for Viraj and me, I thought instead of cooking in between we could just heat the food and eat it. When we took a break, Viraj happily heated the food and plated it, while I raided Naman's fridge to find some soft drinks. He had started stocking them up for us since he learned I didn't drink any hard drinks and Viraj had also turned teetotaller. Viraj mentioned that now that he was earning, he was buying the groceries for the house too because there was no way to pay back to Naman.

"The food is so good!" Viraj mumbled and kept eating the fried rice I had brought while pushing the chapatis to my side.

"Give me some rice!"

"No, I am eating the fried rice, you eat roti and sabzi today!"

I frowned, did he like fried rice so much? I shrugged and ate quietly. I wasn't fussy about food and I only made variety because my little sis was a big drama queen and a foodie.

Later at night, Ana came into the kitchen as I was readying dinner.

"Trish, what had you done with fried rice today?"

I smiled at the memory of Viraj loving it so much that he didn't give me even a morsel to taste.

"What?" I feigned ignorance.

"You added salt twice or thrice in it, I think. I just couldn't eat at all. Threw it away and had to manage with just the roti and sabzi!"

I froze.

He ate the extra salty fried rice because he didn't want me to realize my mistake or make a fuss about it. My heart warmed up and I fell some more in love with him. How had I lucked out? How was he so good?

I entered the house to find him tinkering and adjusting the speakers in the living room.

"What are you doing?"

"Will you dance with me?" He asked softly. I laughed as I nodded.

"I love dancing!" I whispered as I put my hand in his and he pulled me close to his body.

"I know, I have a confession to make!"

"What?" I looked up surprised.

"I saw you dancing the first time I ever saw you!"

"When? Where?" I frowned, I never danced anywhere, where had he seen me? "Didn't we first meet at the pharmacy?"

He shook his head.

"I had come to pick Yuvi up from college, the day before his college fest was to start last year, and I saw you - dancing, twirling around wearing a pink coloured floral print Anarkali suit, looking so delicate, beautiful, and absolutely enchanting that I lost my way and just stood watching you!"

I remembered someone watching me, but I had never seen the guy's face. I was surprised to hear this from Viraj.

"I wanted to talk to you, I even came to the college fest to watch you on the stage, but you didn't."

"I just taught them dancing; I wasn't a student!"

"Yeah, I know that now. I searched for you all over Mumbai, going back to his college so many times for the next six months until I saw you at the pharmacy that day and Shlok had to spoil it all for me!"

I laughed.

"And then you started stalking me!"

"Guilty! I couldn't help it. I couldn't get you out of my mind, Trish. Since, that day I saw you in college, dancing and teaching those girls, I stopped my one-night stands because I only wanted you and none of those girls were you!"

"Viraj?"

"Yeah, I am not telling you this to pressure you or to make you feel guilty or anything. I am just telling you because I don't want to keep something from you. I have been smitten for a very long time and that's why initially I was stalking you because I never thought there would be a day when we could be working together or dancing like this in the living room!"

I put my head on his chest where his heart beat erratically and I found my home. This man had been following me, stalking me but at the same time he was changing his wandering ways and turning his life around. He got angry and reacted impulsively all the time but not once had he crossed a line or hurt me intentionally. Even when he stalked me, he maintained his distance and watched me from afar.

Does that matter? Yes, it does because intentions matter and not just the actions and his intentions had never been wrong!

"Come inside, I want to show you something else!"

Viraj took me to his room where four sketchbooks lay on his bed. I happily picked first one, thinking he made new designs but I was blown away looking at it. Pages and pages of my sketches, my face, my dancing stance, my dresses, my *Jhumkas* in my ear, my lips. This man had been so obsessed. He had four thick 300 pages of sketchbooks all containing only my sketches.

"Viraj!"

"This was my only escape, Trish, all those months, when I knew nothing about you when I couldn't find you in this big city. And after you joined work, I couldn't tell you a thing, my attraction, my obsession, and my love grew for you every waking moment and I needed an output, a constructive way to take the obsession out, lest I scare you or do something impulsive. This was my escape, my haven, one thing that gave me creative satisfaction. Even when you were with Alok, you were here with me."

I found myself choked with emotions and melting at his confession. I never thought someone could love me so much in life. I never thought this kind of love even existed outside the fictional world. And I never thought I would be the luckiest girl on this planet to have this wonderful man loving me, devoting himself to me so completely.

I cupped his face with both my palms and touched my lips to his. He groaned and opened his mouth giving my tongue the shelter it sought. His hands went around my back pulling me to him and I surrendered to his warmth.

"Trish! Please allow me to go, Deeksha Di also said I could go!" Ana pouted. She was using all the tactics in her book to make me agree to her demands.

"But Ana!"

"All my friends are going!"

"You know our condition, Ana."

None of her friends were as poor as us. This trip though for only three days was going to cost me almost what I would make in a month or maybe even more, now that I was not working in Rajvansh Group.

"What are you then working for? Why did you have to leave Rajvansh Group?" She snapped at me.

"Ana!" I looked at her horrified.

"I missed attending all the functions at Raima's wedding also, now that my exams are over, let me go!" She was unperturbed by my reaction or even her words.

"I also didn't attend all the functions!"

"But you are such a bore, you were happy about missing them, unlike me! Moreover, I never asked you to not attend."

I froze for a moment. I was a bore to her. I sacrificed my higher studies so she could study, I sacrificed my outings, my fun, my life, so she could live and I was a bore to her now? She blamed me for leaving the Rajvansh group as if I ever had a choice. As if I wanted to leave that company.

I finally relented; I had no more strength to fight her too. I was tired of my responsibilities and all the expectations from me. I allowed her to go, even with a niggling feeling that something would go wrong. She wanted to go for a three-day trip to Aurangabad with her friends because their exams were over and this was the last time some of them would be together. Yuvi was going, so I asked him to take care of my sister and he laughed that most likely she would end up taking care of him.

# CHAPTER SEVENTEEN

# THINGS FALL APART

*Viraj*

My incessant phone ring woke me up and I fumbled to pick it up. The clock showed it was past midnight.

Trisha Calling...

I jerked and sat up straight.

"Trish?"

"Viraj!" She wailed on the other side making me jump out of bed in panic.

"Trish, what happened? Where are you?"

"I need help!"

"Yeah, tell me, what's wrong?"

"Please come!"

"I am coming home."

"No, I am outside!" My heart sank, outside at 12:45 AM. "I will send my location."

"Are you hurt?"

"No! Baba!" She cried and my heart broke for her.

I changed and rushed out of my room to ask Naman that I would take his car but saw he was sitting on the dining chair reading through something.

"Naman, Trisha called, she was crying, something about her father. Can I take your car, please?"

"Yes, of course. Wait, I will come too."

He was a lawyer and we didn't know what exactly had happened. Trisha was crying uncontrollably and, in my haste, to get to her, I had not even asked.

She sat on the footpath of a deserted road with her father lying down, his head on her lap. We both jumped out of the car as soon as we had parked.

"Trish!" She jerked up to realize I was there and her dam broke free. Tears streaked her face making her look so desolate and devastated that my heart broke all over again for her.

"Baba!"

Naman checked for his pulse while I pulled her in a hug, hiding her face in my neck. Naman shook his head and we both knew her dad was no more. Naman arranged for an ambulance and we took him to the hospital, where Naman took over all the formalities, getting doctor's certificate for the death. They had to do an autopsy to determine the cause of death and we made Trisha sign her consent.

When everything was done and they took the body inside for autopsy, we took Trisha back home. It was almost 4 in the morning and she called her elder sister first. Then she asked me to check with Yuvi, where Ana was.

I made the dreaded call and updated Yuvi, they were to return the next morning anyway, so I told him to just take care of Ana and Trisha told not to say a word to her yet. I conveyed the same message. There was no point telling her and freaking her out yet.

Trisha sat in a daze in a dark corner. I made three cups of tea and Naman nudged me to go sit with her, while he stepped outside to stretch his legs. I pulled her close to my body and she slumped against me.

"Our neighbour uncle came at around 11 at night, saying that he had seen Baba slumped outside a liquor shop. So, I rushed out to check on him. The liquor shop owner said he had a lot of money today and had paid almost 10,000 rupees to the shop owner and had been drinking since evening. He was very happy and kept mumbling something about, his life finally being set. I don't understand where he got the money from?"

"Any of your relatives or someone who had taken a loan from your dad?"

"Loan? My dad took loans, and never gave anything. Our relatives abandoned us a long time back when my mom died and dad turned into an alcoholic. I have called so many of them, already, you saw right? I don't think anyone will even turn up for the funeral."

I pulled her closer to me and she crawled into my lap, putting her head on my shoulder.

"I am tired Viraj!"

"Come on, take a nap!" I slowly ran my hand over her head, in her hair.

"No, tired of everything, tired of being the caregiver, tired of being the responsible one, tired of running around, tired of thinking what to do next!"

"Shhh, don't... I am here now, you take rest, I will manage it all."

"Will you manage it all for the rest of my life too?"

"Yes! I will if you let me!"

"Viraj, what would I do without you!" I thought that was very cheesy of her to say but one look at her face and I realized she said it earnestly.

She really meant it and my heart dropped in my chest. I had never seen her so lost, so fragile, not even when she broke up with Alok and I had thought that was the lowest of her life. She was always strong, always in charge and focused, knowing exactly what to do.

"You will never have to do without me, Trish. I promise!" I spoke softly and she closed her eyes and nuzzled her head on my shoulder.

Her tears soaked my shirt but I didn't flinch, I didn't move because her breathing had evened out and finally, she had fallen asleep.

"Trisha!" A tall girl came running inside and froze when she saw me sitting on the floor holding Trish in my arms.

"She just fell asleep." I whispered.

"Viraj?"

I nodded.

"Deeksha, her sister. Were you with her all night?"

"She called me. We took him to the hospital together with Naman, he is outside."

Trisha stirred and sat up when she saw her sister.

"Di!" She wailed, "I couldn't do anything, I couldn't save him either. I am so sorry!"

How could she have saved him anyway?

Why was she taking this guilt upon herself?

"You did your best, Trish! You did your best, there was no way any of us could have saved him."

"He got money from somewhere; I am dreading if he stole. He gave that shopkeeper ten thousand rupees."

"What?" A guy spoke from behind and we all turned. A tall handsome guy stood at the door.

"Jiju!" Trisha stood up and walked up to him and he gathered her in his arms, hugging her, and something twisted in me. But I controlled my impulses, he was Deeksha's husband, Trisha's brother-in-law.

Naman cleared his throat and we looked at him.

"You, okay?" He asked Trisha, who nodded back at him. "I will go check at the hospital and see how long they will take."

"I will come with you!" I stood up.

"No, you stay here, in case they need anything. I will call you!"

The postmortem report also said that – Death was due to overdrinking.

The amount of alcohol in his body was enough to drown a village, was what the doctor had sighed. It didn't help us in any way but thanks to Naman's connections the postmortem was conducted quickly and the body was released to us by the afternoon.

The body was taken back home, Ana was about to reach back. I had been in touch with Yuvi and he had promised that he would bring her home straight.

I stood outside talking to Shlok who had joined us sometime today morning, keeping all his tasks aside, when Ana and Yuvi reached. Ana paused at our sight then she looked at Shlok and her gaze flickered back and forth.

"Hi, Viraj bhaiya?"

"Come!" I put a hand around her shoulder and took her inside. She froze as her gaze fell on the wrapped body and she lunged forward.

Trisha and Deeksha both scrambled to catch her before she fell on her knees in front of her father.

"Baba? What happened?"

"Last night he overdosed, drank too much!" Trisha who had managed to control her sobs said and was rewarded with a slap across her cheek. I stood stumped while Deeksha caught hold of Ana's hands.

"What's wrong with you?"

"Last night and she didn't bother to tell me? The whole world knows and she didn't call me?"

"What would you have done, if you knew, Ana?" Deeksha spoke in a stern voice. "We all decided it was no use telling you till you reached here, any way you were on your way back."

"No use telling me? Was he not my father?" She screamed and hit at Deeksha and Trisha. Rajveer came forward and pulled Ana back.

"Come, Ana, come here, listen to me!"

I looked in shock and my gaze met with Naman who was angry about this whole encounter while Shlok just shrugged.

"Spoilt!" He muttered and I glared at him.

"Trish!" I spoke moving next to her, she still sat stunned in the same position.

"It's my fault, it's always my fault. I couldn't save Mom; I didn't step out early enough then. I couldn't save Dad; I didn't stop him from drinking too much. I didn't inform her, I didn't scare her when she was alone and away, I didn't do anything right!" She mumbled.

Naman and Shlok were by her side in a minute.

"No, you did it all right, Trisha, she is in shock!" Naman cooed.

"You spoiled her too much, that was your only mistake!" Shlok added and earned a glare from Naman and me.

"Who will do the cremation?" The Panditji who was called for the last rites asked as we prepared to take the body to the cremation ground. As Trisha had predicted none of her relatives had reached and it was just a handful of us and some neighbours.

"Rajveer?" Deeksha immediately turned to her husband.

"No!" He looked horrified, "I can't. Both my parents are alive. I can't, you know it, Deeksha, my parents would never allow it."

"But?" Her voice choked with emotions and I had this impulsive urge to protect her somehow.

"Panditji you only do it, take some extra money for it." He continued.

Trisha gasped and I was horrified at his words. How cruel was this!

"I will do it, Panditji." I said, then I turned to Trisha, "You okay with it, right?"

"Or I can also do it, Trisha is like my little sister, so I can do it as her brother." Naman spoke looking at Trisha and Deeksha. Ana was back in the room and she had apologized to both her sisters for lashing out at them, but Shlok and Naman were pissed at her.

Trisha looked between me and Naman and fresh new tears leaked out of her eyes.

She nodded.

"Let me do this for her, bro!" I whispered to Naman and he nodded. I was glad Naman had accepted Trisha as one of us and was willing to do this for her.

After we returned from the cremation ground the neighbours left, and so did Rajveer and Deeksha, because he made a big fuss that she couldn't stay overnight here and his parents would then be alone at home. I stayed back with Trisha and Ana, while Naman went back home to bring some dinner for us all.

Initial few days, as per their customs, they couldn't cook at home, nor could they order food from restaurants. Now that I had performed the cremation and final rites, I couldn't move out of the house till the next *Havan* was done, for which the sisters decided to do it on the 4th day as per the guidance given by Panditji.

None of their relatives had bothered to come, they all called Deeksha or Trisha and made some excuses. Both the girls were so distraught that after a while they stopped picking up their phone calls too. Deeksha promised her sisters that she would come the next morning and that they could call her anytime, they wanted to talk. I felt her misery shake me, how could her husband not allow her to stay back with her sisters and grieve the loss of a parent? Who was he to allow or not allow in the first place? I vowed in my heart to never take that liberty with Trisha. She should be the one to be able to choose and make her decisions.

Being the male member of this family, Rajveer should have stayed here and taken care of the girls, if I was not in the scene, would these two be left alone on their own? I shuddered at that thought.

I decided to work from her home for the next few days, as the launch was approaching and though the designs were ready and the dresses were being manufactured currently, I just needed to focus on all the co-ordination for the launch party and with the suppliers to ensure the stores we had shortlisted were stocked in time for the launch.

I was also working on my next collection but that was early stages of designing and that was one thing I could do from anywhere as long as I had my sketchbook and pencils.

"It hurts!" Trisha whispered as we lay on the mattress outside in the living room.

Their house was one bedroom flat and the two sisters slept in the room together while I had settled on the mattress that was laid down for the night.

I pulled her closer to me and tucked her under my arms.

"Talk to me, Trish! Speak whatever your thoughts are, empty your mind." She turned around hugging me and burying her face in my throat.

"He was a wonderful father till my mom was alive, after that his guilt ate him from within and he began to drink even more. In his drunken state, he would often yell, hit us, or shout at us and make a ruckus but that was not him, that was his anger, his helplessness, and his inability to save Mom or himself. I made him promise me often that he would reduce drinking and when he was sober, he was good to us. He wasn't a bad man, Viraj!"

"I know sweetheart!" I tucked her close, she needed all the warmth and understanding at this moment.

He was gone now, there was no point thinking that what he did was right or wrong, he needed to rest in peace, and the ones he had left behind needed to heal and overcome this pain. I was here to ensure Trisha didn't bottle up this pain or break down completely. I would do anything to help her get over this grief. The sense of loss would always remain but the pain had to diminish and the guilt should never even cross her mind.

Her confession from yesterday shook me really bad when she acknowledged how she was tired of bearing all the responsibilities and then when she mumbled that anything she did was never enough, I could feel her pain and I had this immense urge to take that horrible feeling of loneliness, guilt, and tiredness away from her.

I wanted her to be happy, and genuinely carefree, that's what most girls her age were, but not her. She took on huge responsibilities early on and she forgot how to live, she was a giver by nature, and she put everyone else first before herself. Everyone's needs before her needs and she just sacrificed so much, her studies, her happiness, her life in a way and still was not appreciated enough. I was determined to change that, even if I was the only one to do so.

She had felt overwhelmed that one time when I had tried to prioritize her wishes and I silently vowed to always prioritize her, make her feel cherished and loved. She was my queen, my whole world and she deserved to be treated like one.

She turned over and I thought she would move away but she surprised me when she snuggled closer to me her back pressing into my front and her soft scent of green apples filled my senses and brought calm to my heart, a welcome feeling of fresh spring.

"I love you, Trish! I love you, even more knowing what you do for your family, what you have done these past few years."

"It was nothing, anyone would do just that!"

"No, not everyone would be able to take on the responsibility, that role at such a tender age that you took on. But now, you are not alone, you have me with you. Will you let me be by your side always?"

"Yes, I would love that!" She turned such that she lay flat on her back, her head resting on my outstretched hand.

"I promise!"

"And I promise to be by your side forever, Viraj! I love you so much!"

"As long as we are together and support each other, I am not saying the going would be smooth or there won't be any problems ever but we would be able to navigate out of it easily."

"I know! At least we won't be lonely, scared that we may do something wrong. The difficult times also feel conquerable if you can lean on someone!"

I kissed her forehead, yes, that was my brave girl reaching out to me, willing to share her burdens, her triumphs, and her life with me!

I performed all the rites for a man, I had only once met and hated that day, like his son. I was not doing it for him, per se, I was doing this for Trisha and I would do it all over again without a pause. My dad had called and hollered on the phone when he heard what I had been doing. I think he learned from Shlok's dad. And I told him, very nicely to mind his own business.

Yuvi kept visiting the sisters often, he was Ana's rock and they were close. It showed in their interactions and I wondered if they were more than friends. I asked Trisha and she looked at me thoughtfully before shrugging and confirming that she doubted the same often.

Naman and Shlok stood by me during this time like a rock. They both wholeheartedly accepted Trisha and agreed with me that I was right in doing what I was doing. Shlok's mom sent food for the day, we had the *havan* at home, when she learned I was at Trisha's house. She was an angel and I never understood why she stayed so aloof and away from her own son's life.

I had grown close to both of her sisters too, I cared for them all. Trisha had once asked me that she was a package deal and I accepted it wholeheartedly. Of course, I left my family behind but that was my choice, I would happily embrace her family, her friends like she had embraced Yuvi, Shlok and Naman, the only ones who mattered to me.

I took Ana to the college for her admission in post-graduation, as Trisha had not been feeling very well since last night. I think she was finally coming down with a fever or something and we decided to let her rest, while we could finish up the college formalities.

Just as we were stepping out of the college after finishing up our work, I heard someone call my name and turned, just in time to catch Vandana, who came running over to hug me.

"Vandana!"

"Bhaiya, I miss you so much!" I put her down and pecked her forehead. She was and will always remain my little princess.

"Vandana, do you know Ana?"

"Yeah, she is in Yuvi bhaiya's class." Vandana was a year younger than Yuvi.

Both the girls hugged each other warmly when I heard another voice and stiffened.

"Hello, hello, who do we have here?" Rohit came to a stop in front of me. He must be here for Vandana.

"Hi, how are you?" Ana spoke before I could respond and I looked at her. How did she know him?

"I am good, angel, how are you?" He grinned at her with glassy eyes.

Was he lusting after both the sisters?

"How do you know each other?"

"We have met, a few times!" Rohit said non-committal and I left it at that. We spoke for a while and then took our leave.

"How do you know him?"

"He often comes to our college, for Vandana I suppose. He first spoke to me a couple of months back and said that he worked with you and Trish and was very impressed with her work."

"Hmmm, okay!" I didn't have a nice feeling about it all and she confirmed.

"Can I ask you something?"

"Sure."

"But you have to promise not to say a word to Trish!"

"Okay, what is it?"

"Why did Trish leave Rajvansh group? Because you left right?"

I laughed.

"It's the other way around actually. She never left, my dad forced her to leave because he didn't like the fact that I was getting close to your sis, and when I confronted my dad, he kicked me out too."

"Oh!"

"Why?"

"Rohit told me, that Trisha was a good performer but, in her haste, to seduce you, she quit as soon as you left the company and spun off this different tale to tell me and Di."

"What?" I knew Rohit was up to something. The way he was smiling at Ana was not right.

"Ana, I know Rohit and I are cousins and practically both are strangers for you, but can you do me a favour, please?"

"To not talk to Rohit?"

"Yes, please! Ask me or Yuvi if you want clarification, you trust Yuvi, right? But Rohit tried to intimidate your sister, tried to force her and when she didn't respond to his wooing, he complained to my dad that she was trying to woo both of us."

Ana gasped.

"You know your sister is better than that!"

She nodded lost in her thoughts.

# LEARNING TO GROW

*Trisha*

I stepped out of the house looking like a princess, feeling like one too holding Viraj's hands. He had designed this dark bottle green full-length gown for me, to wear for our first collection launch. It was a dual party of sorts, the launch of our company and our new collection in collaboration with the French brand we had been in discussions with for months now. Viraj looked stylishly dapper as he was dressed in a Black Tuxedo, that Yuvi had managed to sneak out of his room along with a lot of other items that belonged to him over the months.

All our hard work would be presented to the world and our fate as newbie designers would be decided as the world of fashion may love it or thrash it.

It had been two weeks since my father passed away and the numbness just wouldn't go. Since the time we returned from his cremation, I had not even stepped out of the house. Everyone else had but something within me shattered that night. I had been trying so hard and for so long to get him to stop drinking, we had even enrolled him in the rehab centre, couldn't get the treatment started only because of lack of funds.

After I lost my mom, the way I did, I had tried to take on the role of both parents in the house, caring for Ana and sometimes Di and dad as well, like mom would and earning for the household like dad should have. I put my own life on pause to take up multiple roles that time demanded of me and that night as I sat with his dead weight in my lap, everything, every illusion that I had created that it would all turn out fine in the end lay shattered all around me.

A piece of me died that night with him, a helplessness took hold of me when I realized whatever I wanted to do for him was just mere words, and I couldn't do a thing. When time came, I was late yet again. I stepped out of the house late when Mom lay dead outside, maybe, just maybe if I had come out as soon as Dad had pushed her out, I could have saved her.

Similarly, if I had come out sooner to look for Dad instead of eating my dinner and drawing up sketches, maybe I could have saved him too. I was late yet again, and I felt I was drowning under the weight of this guilt. I couldn't face Di or Ana; hence I had turned to the only other person I knew I could depend on.

Viraj and Naman came and just took over all the formalities, all the responsibilities that ideally would have befallen me but I was too shattered to protest or ask them if they needed anything. They both cared for me, and I knew in my heart they were doing it all for me, not for the dead man and some where I was glad, I felt relieved. I had someone.

Both of them stood by me like a rock, Shlok and Yuvi also did a lot, I am not saying they didn't, but Naman and Viraj went over and beyond. They paused their own lives to help me, to sort out my mess. If I was stepping into the party tonight, it was thanks to these guys, these four pillars I had found recently and they were now my biggest support system.

Deeksha Di had her own life, her own challenges and she was always torn between her duties as a daughter and daughter-in-law before and now struggled to keep up as a sister too, and I understood that. I urged her to choose her in-laws at times, because that was what was expected of her, and she was always a stickler to follow the rules and do what was expected of her. I knew she loved me to bits and was always cheering for me, tonight I had pleaded with her and Jiju to come for the launch, it would mean the world for me to see happiness in their eyes.

Ana was still a kid, I felt. She was moody, she threw tantrums and she made it all up within minutes. I was shocked when she had accused me upon seeing our father's dead body but she quickly apologized. She was impulsive, she acted before she thought and we understood her. Mom was snatched away from her early on and now dad. Of course, she felt cheated, she felt alone and she lashed out.

But these handful of people were my tribe, my only people. No one else mattered, well I had no one else. Not a single relative from either my mom's side or my dad's side had bothered to come down for the funeral or any of the rituals later as well. An aunt who lived in Mumbai had turned up for about half an hour, ate lunch, and left. Deeksha Di mentioned that not counting anyone as a relative was better than having these kinds of people around, we were better off without them. Expectations always caused grief and hurt. And she was right!

The launch party was a big success as a few big names of the business industry, fashionistas, and even Bollywood stars showed up. Viraj and I took centre stage as he announced the launch of our brand, our new collection and also spoke a little bit about our next upcoming Wedding Collection and dropped the hint that we were open for collaborations for it. He had earned himself a lot of respect in the past year as the CEO of Rajvansh Group with his fresh style of leading the decades-old business.

A lot of businessmen were inspired by his fresh approach while some old-school men also hated him. The reasons for his split with Rajvansh Group were kept under wraps thankfully and that aura of mystery surrounded him too. Not one member of his family was invited other than Yuvraj and he showed up looking devilishly handsome in a navy-blue suit, which he joked he got stitched especially for tonight.

A famous jewellery designer approached Viraj to discuss a potential tie-up. To use his jewellery for our upcoming wedding collection and Viraj introduced me to him. We spoke for a while and decided to meet the coming week at a café. We mentioned that we were yet to open our office and worked out of home. This was overheard by another business magnate who offered us a floor in his new corporate office building that was opening up next month. He said he was looking for some fancy names and brands to take up the office space and rental could well be negotiated.

Viraj took his business card and hope bloomed in my chest. It was all thanks to Viraj's name, and his goodwill in the business industry that people were ready to support even his new brand, else fashion industry was such a cut-throat business that I had heard people only brought others down and never lifted anyone.

The next three months proved to be hectic, bone-breaking tiring yet amazing for us and our brand. We were able to move into a swanky new office space, which was a store in the front and an office at the back, with huge space for designing and storage of raw materials. Our next collection was almost ready and we had finalized several businesses to tie up with for this collection.

Viraj had recently started taking customized designing orders, where the actual good moolah was as per him, because only the uber-rich came to him for their designer wear, and income from just two or three such orders in a month was enough for us to pay the rent for this swanky place. Any more orders that we received were straightaway saving or profit as you call it.

I was learning the ropes of business from him all over again, my BBA degree being put to use at times too and Viraj was an amazing mentor. Now that Ana was busy with her post-graduation, and I had fewer responsibilities, I was able to spend more time with him at work and off work.

He had moved out of Naman's house last month and had rented an apartment, a two-bedroom place, very close to our store. There was a penthouse in the same building which Viraj was eyeing. Naman and Shlok had offered to loan him the money to buy it before it got taken away by someone else, but he didn't agree. He said if it was meant for him, he would be able to earn, save, and buy it on his own.

The property prices in Mumbai were sky-high and my heart jumped in my throat every time these guys started discussing buying a property, a house, or a farmhouse. But I had faith in Viraj, I knew he would soon be able to manage it. He had come a long way in the past six months since he separated from Rajvansh Group. Managing to create a designer label and brand by oneself was not easy and he had done it by sheer hard luck, dedication, and passion for his craft. I was so glad; that I had been able to contribute a little bit to his wonderful journey and that he was mine!

"Trish, you decide!"

"What?" I sat up straight, I was lost in my thoughts and was not even listening to their banter when Shlok took my name.

"Where to go for a holiday, you both deserve one and we are determined to crash it for you guys!"

I laughed at his words.

"I don't know!"

"One place, you have always wanted to go?" Viraj turned to me. He knew I had barely travelled and that I wanted to see the world.

"You know what, let's go to Goa, she hasn't been to Goa!" Naman said.

"You haven't been to Goa? Yeah, let's go, let's drive down, even more fun!" Shlok said excitedly.

And they all got busy discussing Goa holiday plans and when would be a good time. Soon, all three brought out their phone calendars and discussion began in earnest. I slowly stepped away to prepare dinner for all of us. I loved to cook for these guys because they loved everything I made and the way they attacked the food, I felt a satisfaction deep within that they were cherishing something

I had created. Even if I gave them burnt rice, I was sure, these three would polish it off and ask if there was any more of it!

No tantrums, no fuss, they only showered me with love and care. All three of them were poles apart, while Viraj was mine, heart, and soul, Naman was the quiet, observant guy, who weighed his words, thought equally with his heart and mind, and was always there for those he cared for. Shlok hid behind his façade of easy-going, flamboyant Casanova image but deep within I always felt he hid a lot of pain and longing. He laughed easily, played around, and had a great sense of humour too.

Viraj had called me in the morning to say he had to meet some potential client and wouldn't be coming into the office early, so without pressing for any more info, I went ahead and opened the store. We had hired two people to manage the store starting this month, because we had a good footfall and we didn't want to miss out on our designing or creation time when we were waiting on customers.

I sat at my desk designing a flared pant suit with a draped dupatta, when I felt warm breath on my neck and turned to see a smiling Viraj looking down at the design.

"This looks amazing, what shades are you thinking of?"

"I am thinking of bold darker shades for this because this a statement piece, not everyone will dare to wear this for a wedding festivity but those who will, would surely want to stand out!"

"Perfect! I think a dark orange?"

"Yeah, and dark purple, not magenta but a darker shade of violet, you know more towards blue tinge."

"I get what you mean, in fact peacock blue would also look nice and the material?"

"This has to be silk, actually Tussar silk so that it would retain the flare, shape and cut."

"Hmmm..." He picked up the design and looked at it closely.

"Where were you all morning?"

"Doing so many things darling, so many!" He laughed and pulled me in a for a warm kiss.

I always melted against him, every time he touched me or kissed me. He had stayed true to his promise and did nothing more than kissing, touching, and cuddling with me. He had explored some more of my body in the past few months but never went all the way.

Then and there I decided that it was to change. We were both committed to this relationship and I was sure he loved me like no one ever could. The lengths he had already gone to for me, were unparalleled and I could never find anyone better or more suited than him.

I didn't think I was capable of loving anyone else anymore either. He was so much like me, he understood me completely. He understood my wishes and my thoughts even before I could voice them. He had made it a mission to make me a priority in his life. I had never felt so loved and so treasured in my life before him.

The next day after we closed the store, I asked him if he was okay for me to come over to his place and he was happy to hear it. As we entered our house, that's what he always called it, our first home. I hugged him from behind, he stilled.

"What's wrong?"

"What? Can I not hug my love?" I pouted and he chuckled.

"Then let me also hug my love!" He held my hands to loosen the grip and slowly turned around to hug me but I went on my tiptoes to kiss him and he welcomed my tongue in his mouth with a loud groan. I pushed him back and he started walking backwards towards the bedroom. The kiss was hot and melting my insides.

I tugged at his t-shirt and he lifted his arms to let me remove it. I had seen him shirtless before and I loved his chiselled form, his muscled shoulders and arms, his perfect abs felt so good under my fingers. I traced his biceps with my fingers and he shut his eyes close to savour the feeling. A calm fell over his face and he surrendered to cherishing the onslaught I was bringing to his body. I could see he was enjoying it far too much by the tent that was threatening to form in his jeans.

I trailed my hands over his abs, his flat stomach and moved closer to the waistline. I flipped his jeans button open and his eyes shot open.

"Trish!"

"I want you, Viraj!"

He gulped.

"Don't Trish, I crave for you so bad, I won't be able to hold back!"

"Then don't! Make my yours?"

His eyes darkened as my words registered in his mind.

"We are in our home, we are together, we love each other, what is stopping you now?"

"Oh, I am only waiting for you, waiting for you to be comfortable! I don't want to rush into this, because I love you for you, not for your body!"

"You don't love my body!" I feigned shock.

"I haven't seen it yet!" He laughed and then sobered as he realized what he had said.

I pulled my t-shirt over my head and stood in front of him in my bra and jeans.

His Adam's apple bobbed as his gaze fell on my exposed body. I wore a simple cotton black bra, I only had these.

"Can I?" He whispered before slowly trailing his finger on my skin along the edge of the bra and I shuddered. He looked into my eyes, seeking permission to touch me and I nodded for him to go on and explore. There was nothing more I wanted right now.

He slowly trailed his finger along the bra line and then pulled it down to uncover my left breast and crash his lips on it making me groan loudly. He chuckled as he teased my pebbled nip with his mouth and tongue, then he bit it slightly and immediately licked it making me shudder. My legs felt like jelly and I grabbed onto his shoulders tighter fearing I would fall. He understood my plight and moved me back to the bed, laying me down gently before lowering himself on me.

He waited for me to give him the go-ahead and I pushed my body up to touch his invitingly. His hand snaked behind my back and he flipped the bra open in a swift move, peeling it away from my body and admiring my naked self warmly. His mouth went back to work on my right nip and I was transported to heaven.

Oh my God! This felt so good, he had a magical mouth.

He laughed and I realized I had probably said it out loud.

"Wait till you see the real magic of my mouth!" He left my breasts alone and trailed his mouth down my stomach dropping open-mouthed soft kisses, licking, and trailing his lips all over eliciting a whimper of joy from me.

"Tell me you want this, Trish! Let me touch you?" He had paused his exploration at my waist where my jeans sat untouched.

"I want this, I want you!"

He dipped his tongue in my navel and that was the most exotic sensation I had ever felt, I wanted him to not stop ever. Oh, I could live in this bliss forever. His hands trailed down and he slowly pulled my jeans down inch by inch his gaze feasting on me as he unwrapped me slowly. Then he did the same with my cotton panties and his eyes went feral as his gaze fell on my core. He touched me tenderly, reverentially then bent his head to sniff me.

"What are you doing?"

"Relax! I won't bite." He looked up and the smile from his face was wiped out when he realized no one had ever gone down on me.

He kissed me, slowly pushing a finger inside and I jumped on the bed, making him shoot his left hand out to hold me down.

"I will be gentle, sweetheart, trust me!"

"I trust you!" I whispered back.

He kissed my core as his fingers worked magic and I felt a fresh tightening in my stomach as if he was tying me up in some unseen knots. I didn't understand why my body was responding the way it was - clenching and tightening demanding more of this awesome sensation then my body gave way to complete surrender and I saw stars behind my shut eyes as I thought I was falling freely down from heaven.

"Oh, oh Viraj!"

I lay there panting hard as he looked up at me, my juices all over his mouth!

"Delicious!" Was all he said as he moved up to kiss me hard and I tasted myself.

"That was my first orgasm!" I whispered wanting to share with him and he frowned then hugged me close.

"Want another?"

I nodded and then I remembered I was being greedy and I had not helped him find his release yet. I wanted him to see the stars and have his orgasm as good as I just had.

"With you, in me!"

He smiled as he stood up, I sat up to help him remove his jeans and his boxer shorts. Oh God, his length was hard like steel, smooth and big, was this even going to fit inside? I worried about the pain it would bring along. He worked magic with fingers but this was surely going to hurt. I moved forward to kiss the tip of his length and he shuddered. If just a touch caused this reaction, I was tempted to see what taking his length in my mouth would do to him. I covered my lips on him and he groaned.

"Oh Trish! I will blow up!" He grunted as I licked him and moved my mouth up and down his length taking it in deeper and deeper. "Wait! Wait! Stop."

I stopped alarmed.

"You don't like it?"

"Oh, I like it too much, but I want to go in."

I moved back and he climbed on the bed and hovered over me, balancing himself on his elbows. He moved his fingers down my core as he crashed his mouth on mine. I moaned as his mouth and fingers assaulted my senses yet again. I was drenched once again and he slowly pushed his length in me slightly. I stilled and he paused.

"Relax, relax your muscles, I won't hurt!"

I did as he cooed and he pushed another inch in and I realized that no pain shot up. I relaxed further and he moved in again. Inch by inch he pushed his length in and my body stretched and adjusted to his girth. He felt so good, why had I been scared of this? He was so careful, so gentle. He moved slowly pulled out his length and pushed it hard in one stroke and I moaned in ecstasy.

"So good, Trish, you are so tight! Is it hurting?" He looked at me and our gaze met.

"No, this feels so good, you feel so good!" I moaned.

He kissed my forehead and started moving slowly at first then increasing his pace, setting us up at a wonderful pace as he began the eternal dance of mating and I clenched hard around him eliciting a groan from him. He bit my ear and that was my undoing, I crashed down the biggest wave that was there in the sea and he followed me behind with one last stroke. We both tightened our grips on each other as we crashed the conjugal wave of ecstasy, and pure love.

He kissed all over my face as he slowly pulled out.

Then he froze.

"Shit, Trish, I am so sorry, I forgot the protection!" He panicked and I realized I didn't even think of protection, one thing I had been so careful about with Alok.

"I have never done without protection before!" I blurted.

"Neither have I. How did I forget? You will need to take the pill after."

I nodded, though I was due to get my periods in two days. This should be safer time of the month.

"I am sorry!" His worried gaze met mine.

"I am not, it was so good, so worth it!"

"It was too good, I agree, I have never come so hard and I have never felt this connected before."

"I dreaded this because with him, I would only get hurt and it pained me. I never felt good."

"Because you are mine, you wouldn't like it with anyone else!"

I laughed.

"It's supposed to feel good; he was an idiot to not have taken care of you before himself!"

He pulled me in a hug and then picked me up to take me to the shower to clean me up under the warm water. Well, he cleaned me but dirtied me further first. His logic being one time or twice wouldn't matter now that I had to take the pill anyway.

I was about to confide in Deeksha Di the next time we met but she beat me to it, she mentioned that she felt super sore because they were both trying to conceive a child for a few months now, to no luck. So, Jiju had been pushing her for intercourse every day and she always said it hurt her. Was Jiju also being selfish like Alok, I thought but couldn't ask because asking this meant me telling her about my multiple orgasms, and when she was worried, I didn't want her to worry about one more thing.

Her mother-in-law had started telling her to get herself checked and she was super stressed about it these days. She was getting desperate and was even ready to get herself checked. I was the one telling her to try naturally and not get doctors involved.

"Let's go out for dinner tonight?" Viraj asked as we were eating our lunch.

"Out, where?"

"I never got to take you out anywhere to nice places for lunch or dinner dates, to cafes, I never had money but now I want to Trish, please don't say no!"

I chuckled and nodded.

"Let me make reservations!" He picked his phone excitedly. "Dress in your best!"

"Best?"

"Yeah, I am taking you to a new fancy place. Let's wine and dine in style for once!"

I laughed at his words but agreed.

If these things gave him joy, I was all for it and it was true we had never gone on any dates or lunches or dinners outside. I was always broke and when he had the money, we weren't together and when he became as penniless as me, all we could manage was the simplest of home food, no ordering in or fancy dinners.

I dressed in my best party dress that I owned, Viraj had designed this as well for me, a dark blue calf-length dress made of light chiffon material with silk lining, which clung to my body perfectly making me feel like a model. Ana helped me with light makeup, I was still not good at it and she had started taking a lot of interest in all this in the past few months.

"Ana, is there someone I should know about?" Suddenly the idea popped into my head and she froze, she blushed profusely but shook her head.

"Ana?"

"No, there is no one, I will tell you if there was someone!"

But her not meeting my gaze told me something was fishy. I decided not to press the issue and left her on her own. She was doing her post-graduation in commerce and also taking Chartered Accountancy exams, which were no easy feat. Yuvi was also in her class and I wondered if he would know anything about her crush or boyfriend. Was Yuvi her...? No, but they were good friends or were they more?

Viraj had finally bought a car earlier this month, after saving up enough. He was just not made for travelling in cabs, metros or even my bike for that matter. He had tried when he had no other option but he was too much of a clean freak. He loved his wheels and had bought a magnificent-looking black Kia Carens this time around. Of course, he couldn't afford a Merc yet but this was progress.

"Where are you lost?" He asked me as we stopped at a signal.

"This was the signal where I had that accident." I replied reminiscing those days. How I had frantically called Alok, who had kept rejecting my calls. Then I called Viraj and he showed up within a few minutes, without asking any questions or thinking of spoiling his evening for me.

"Yeah, that reminds me, I forgot to follow up on it, Naman was pursuing the case for a very long time, these CCTVs were out of order that day, else we would have found the culprit long back."

"It was just an accident am sure, someone lost control and couldn't apply the brake on time. Leave it!"

"No, someone deliberately followed you and hit your bike and zoomed off. It was a black car, high-end one too, but we couldn't get the full number plate from anybody."

"Oh! I remember seeing a small scratch at the back as the car sped off, on the corner of the back bumper. It was small but I remember the shape of it."

"Okay, draw it for me, please!"

I nodded, wondering why I hadn't thought of it earlier.

Viraj took me inside to the rooftop hotel and the view blew my mind. I squealed in delight. He had booked a corner table for us with the best view of the city beneath us and the star-sprinkled sky above us. The food was said to be delicious and I asked him to order for both of us. I was not at all fussy about food and he knew international cuisines far better than I did anyway.

While he ordered I asked for a piece of paper and pen and drew up the shape of that scratch as I remembered from the time I had fallen on the road and my bike had taken the brunt of the impact. It had taken more than three weeks to get it repaired, repainted, and get it back. I showed it to him and he frowned thinking long and hard.

"I know it's just a scratch and not a sticker but it is a weird shape and looks like I have seen this before!"

After we finished our dinner, he ordered Tiramisu for dessert because I loved it. Just as the cake arrived, the manager arrived to ask me for feedback on the food and ambiance and spoke to me for about two minutes. When he left, I sighed and turned around only to gasp in surprise.

Viraj was down on one knee in front of me holding a glittering solitaire ring in his right hand.

"Trisha, you already know how much I love you but what you may not know is that you make me a better man. You know I can go to any lengths for your wishes but what you may not know is that you also ground me, center me, and calm me. You are the most treasured person in my life and I want to spend the rest of my life with you, treasuring you, cherishing you, making you insanely happy, and loving you till my last breath. Will you let me have this responsibility to help you fulfill each of your dreams and aspirations? Will you let me walk with you on this beautiful journey to success? Will you marry me and make me complete?"

Tears appeared in my eyes and I quickly blinked them away.

"I will, a thousand times I will marry you, Viraj, I love you so much! You are my most precious!"

He slid the ring on my finger and leaned forward to seal the deal with a kiss.

CHAPTER NINETEEN

# TAKING THE PLUNGE

*Viraj*

My phone rang just after I had turned the car around, dropping Trisha back home after our wonderful dinner.

She said Yes!

But I was confident that she would say yes, though I had a little jittery nervousness. I had already checked in the Marriage Registrar's office in Bandra about the process of the court marriage and was now determined to take Trish there within a day or two so we could apply for the notice to be generated. I knew my dad wouldn't like the marriage or might want to oppose it, but that was okay, I didn't care, I just hoped the news didn't reach his ears.

"Hello Naman?"

"Hey buddy, where are you? Can you come home, now?"

"Yeah, sure, I can be there in about 15 minutes, am on the road."

"Come, there is something!"

"What?"

"You proposed to Trisha?"

"Yeah, how do you know?" I frowned; how did he guess this?

"Your pictures are on social media and some had really nasty captions, I am working with the media houses to get that cleaned up, as we speak now."

"Shit, I am coming!"

Shlok had reached Naman's house by the time I entered and I saw both of them making frantic calls on my behalf. I waited till they finished to update me.

"So, someone clicked a photo of you proposing, down on your knees and put it on social media with the caption – **"A low-class tramp finds her prince charming in disowned Rajvansh Heir. Is this why the heir got disowned?** ... yeah!" Naman mentioned.

I paled at the words; how could anyone stoop so low? And why? Just to get more traffic on their post?

"We have got it changed to read – **"True love always wins. The most eligible bachelor of town is now taken!"** Some were insistent on adding Rajvansh heir tag to you, so for them, we got it changed to – **"Rajvansh heir finds his match in a talented designer and makes her not just life partner but business partner too! They recently launched their brand – Virsha.".** Sounds, okay?" Shlok read from a sheet of paper they both had in front of them.

I simply nodded. I couldn't believe how vile some people could be and sent a quiet prayer that I had these two watching my back.

"Viraj, you won't believe who was behind this?"

I froze, did they find that already?

"Who?" I dreaded the answer that it was my father.

"Rohit Rajvansh! And I have just got proof that he and your dad were both seen in Trisha's locality on the day her father died."

I slumped into a nearby chair and Shlok pushed his beer bottle in front of me. I looked at it, almost reaching out then I remembered, this was what Trisha hated and I shook my head. This was what had snatched both her parents away from her, and I could never ever take even a drop of it, for her sake, for my sake!

"Has it been cleaned up from social media completely? I don't want Trisha or Ana to see this!"

"Yes, it has been. We also released an official statement on your behalf to media groups along with this photo, so it should be okay. I have people checking if there is any more site running anything other than what we are feeding them." Naman spoke, he had contacts in media and investigative agencies. Being a top-notch Criminal lawyer came with its perks too.

"Thanks, bro, I owe you one!"

"Never mind."

"Did you not see Rohit or anyone related to him in the restaurant?" Shlok asked.

I shook my head, frankly, I had not even bothered to take my eyes off Trisha to look around or notice anyone. I had been so enchanted by her, as she drew the design on the paper.

"Naman, I got this for you, Trisha remembered the car that hit her bike, had this weird-shaped scratch at the back. It was a black car and she had noticed this, as she fell." I remembered just in time to pass him the paper and both of them peered at it.

"I will pass it on to my investigator, but this I doubt would be of any help!"

"I know, it's a long shot. Anyway, what do we have on Rohit?"

"A CCTV footage where he is seen in that locality and trying to look for someone. I am trying to get more footage and see if he met her father."

"Someone gave her father 10,000 rupees that day which made him drink so much!" I reiterated mindlessly, though I couldn't understand why Rohit would want to give Trisha's dad that money.

"Yeah, you told me, 10,000 for Rohit is no big deal, and that's what my theory is!"

"But I thought Rohit was close to you?"

"Yeah, he was he has always been but he loved the power our surname brought too, more than I did. He had been working hard to shine in my dad's eyes for years. His dad never held power in the company, and my dad didn't give him any, but Rohit was determined from early on to change that, he wanted equal power as me. And I saw it, and gave him that, CFO position because he was capable and I didn't want any negativity cropping up later either."

"Right!" Naman nodded.

"If Rohit could leak the photo to media, and pay money to Trish's dad, he could as well have hired someone for her accident."

I gulped as Shlok's words sank in. No, my heart leaped, Rohit would never do that, hurt someone intentionally. But then my mind did agree that yes, he could have, just out of spite, but why? At that time Trisha and I were not together. I saw him look at Trisha and was it possible that he was also interested in her, he had implied that to her. He had asked her to lavish him with attention too.

"What now?" Shlok looked up when all three of us sat lost in our own thoughts.

"I will take Trisha to apply for court marriage tomorrow itself."

"Oh, lover boy, I meant what now about Rohit! Every chance you get you jump back on Trisha!" Shlok lamented sarcastically and Naman laughed.

"I foresee opposition from my dad!"

"I will see if something can be done about it." Naman replied.

The next day I pulled Trisha in my arms while we were in our office and asked her,

"What kind of a wedding do you want?" I had updated her about the social media fiasco later at night, just in case she came across any news or wondered why our photos were on all news portals.

She looked at me surprised as her hands went around my neck.

"We are getting married, right?" I asked suddenly feeling worried.

"Yeah, are we getting married so soon?"

"You want to wait?"

"Yes, no, I mean, I never thought of it."

"I asked you last night if you remember whether you would marry me and you said yes, right?"

"Of course, I remember and I will marry you, I just didn't process that we would be discussing this so soon. I mean you are right, we should, we are practically together all day, might as well be together at night."

"Oh yes, every night, you and me in the same bed!"

She blushed and I laughed. How I loved to tease her and see her getting all flustered!

"We might have to move Ana into the spare bedroom, you do realize that right when we get married and I move out of that house?"

I nodded, I knew she would ask for it and I was okay with it. She was responsible for Ana and so was I, going forward. I wouldn't wash my hands off the sisters like Rajveer had.

"Of course, Ana will stay with us, we can't leave her all alone in that house!"

"Are you sure, Viraj, I come with a lot of baggage!"

"Shhh, that's not baggage, Trish, that's your family, your sisters, and I am more than happy to have them stay with me, I have grown up in a joint family and I liked it, you know my aunt brought me up far more than my mother, so am all for it. Right now, I have no one to call my family except you and Yuvi and I am more than happy to have Ana and Deeksha included in my family, if they would let me."

"Oh Viraj, I love you so much!"

"Oh, thank God for that!" I grumbled and she kissed me softly until our new store assistant, Jiya, walked in and we jumped apart.

That night I took Trisha back home, so I could talk to her without disturbances and she mentioned that she didn't want an elaborate wedding, a simple one with just our handful of closest people in attendance. I wanted the same thing and I suggested that we get married in court and she agreed readily.

"Ana? I want to ask you something."

"What bhaiya?"

I had come to drop Trisha home and decided to broach the topic with her too.

"Trisha and I are planning to get married..."

She squealed loudly even before I could finish asking what I wanted and jumped to hug me. I was not prepared for her assault and stumbled back but quickly regained my balance making all of us laugh. She was just a child at times, with her actions and her unbridled enthusiasm.

"Congratulations!"

"Thank you!" I pecked her head to calm her down, "I want you to move in with us, once we are married."

She frowned.

"You are asking the wrong sister!" She grinned.

"No, I am asking you!"

"Why?"

"You think you'll stay here alone? No way, you move in with us, in our rented apartment, it is a two-bedroom house and we can lock up this house."

"But my plants!" She pouted.

"We will take turns, come and water them!"

"No, you both stay there, I can continue here, why should I move? It won't be nice!"

"No, Ana, it won't be safe for you alone here, moreover you have to study. I feel it would be better being together." Trisha spoke.

Ana looked between the two of us and shrugged.

"I need to think about it! What's for dinner today?"

"Why don't you cook something!" I told Ana and she looked at me horrified.

"I am terrible, you sure you don't want to die of food poisoning?"

"And you want to live alone here if you die of your own cooked food, we won't even get to know!" I retorted with a straight face.

Her eyes popped out in shock while Trisha chuckled.

"Fine, fine, I will stay with you both, only till I can learn how to cook. I love my independence way too much!"

Ana was a sassy firecracker and I worried for the guy who would ultimately fall for her and marry her! I looked at Trisha and thanked my stars that I had found an angel and she had fallen in love with me too!

Naman walked into my house grinning late at night.

"I think I have found the solution to one of your problems!"

"And which one is that?"

"Look at this video and you will understand."

I took the phone from his hand and played the video, all colour drained off my face. Shucks! This was the last thing I was expecting.

"This is from yesterday!"

"And today?"

"Home. Never two days in a row!"

"Do we have more footage?"

"Yes, all the way back to two months ago!"

I nodded, then dialled a number. I needed to get this thing cleared once and for all.

"What do you want?" Came the curt response and I put the phone on speaker.

"Hello, Dad! How are you?"

"Let me guess, Viraj, you have finally come to your senses and want to apologize and return home. It took longer than I had anticipated."

"No, Dad, I am not returning home. I called to inform you that I am going to marry Trisha soon!"

After a brief silence, he continued like it was no big deal.

"And you want my blessings?"

"No, I don't want your blessings or your money or anything at all from you. What I want is that you will not meddle in my marriage or my business!"

He chuckled.

"What if I do?"

"I happen to have a few videos of the Taj Hotel lobby and the main entrance."

"What is that?"

"The Taj Hotel, where a very familiar looking man is seen going in and out with a Mrs. Khanna regularly and you know what some of the videos show the man's face very clearly!"

"Are you threatening me?"

"No, I have learnt some trade tricks from you, Dad. I am not threatening you, not yet. I am just informing you that anytime I feel someone is meddling or trying to sabotage my life, my business, or my wife, I can leak these videos to the media anonymously!”

“Viraj!”

“Shhh, shouting is not good for you Dad, imagine if your better half at home, hears you shouting and asks what the matter was?” My voice was menacing and I suddenly remembered how much Trisha had mellowed me down and turned me into a calm person.

“This is blackmailing!”

“Not at all, Dad, your secrets are safe with me, as long as you stay away from me and what’s mine and ask your minion, Rohit to also stay away.”

“Give me those videos, Viraj!”

“Like I said, safe with me, until I feel threatened!”

“I will not let you marry that lowly girl. She is after your money, why don’t you understand?”

“What money Dad, I have nothing, you even took away the money that I had earned, all my personal possessions, what do I have now?”

“You have my name.”

“I will give it up, too!”

“You are committing a blunder, Viraj, you will realize it when she has taken away everything from you!”

“Thanks, but you were the one who took away everything from me, she has only given me till now.”

“I will make sure you both don’t get married!”

“Let’s see how you stop our marriage because right now I have enough videos to break your sham of a marriage and make the share prices of Rajvansh Group crash.”

“Don’t you threaten me, Viraj!”

“Don’t you meddle with what’s mine, Mr. Rajvansh!”

“You will regret this!”

“I won’t flinch before releasing these and you know me. I have lost everything once, but you haven’t. You will regret this if you try to make me choose Trisha over everything else one more time, Mr. Rajvansh, because I will, I always will. I hope we don’t cross each other’s paths.”

"I hope so too. You are the biggest disappointment of my life!"

"Glad to be!" I cut the call.

Naman recorded the phone call, though that was illegal but he was the lawyer and he could manipulate things if they went downhill anyway.

Yuvi rang the bell early the next morning and I frowned when I saw him almost bouncing in joy.

"Congratulations Bhai!"

"Thanks!" I replied confusion written on my face.

"Dad was furious last night and told Mom that you were marrying Trish!"

I smiled.

"I am! I was planning on calling you this evening to tell you about it. We are going for a simple court marriage. And I want you with me!"

"Of course! I will come, you tell me the date and time. I cannot miss it for anything!"

I hugged him. He was a treasure!

"We will take your camera and what are you wearing?"

I chuckled, as he immediately got down to the nitty-gritty of the wedding.

Shlok lay sprawled on the couch while I sat on the rug and Naman sat in the recliner I had just bought.

"We three should dress alike!" Shlok muttered gazing at the ceiling.

"Why? Are all of us getting married?" Naman countered.

"No, but we are best friends. And it's going to be the only wedding."

"Why?" I looked at him, confused.

"I won't marry ever. And Naman won't be able to marry either, his dad is the best divorce lawyer in India, every girl would run away hearing that!"

I laughed while Naman made a face.

"You know what, as a kid I imagined the three of us marrying three best friends!" Naman said softly, as if lost in his childhood fantasy.

"Trish has no friends, right Viraj?" Shlok looked up.

"Yeah, they are three sisters, though!" I said leaning my head on the couch behind me.

"Yeah, one is married and one is a pure devil. No, thank you very much!" Shlok propped himself on his elbow and folded both his hands.

"The devil is so into you, man!" Naman gazed at him and I sat up straight at his words.

"What?" This was enough to make Shlok sit up straight.

"Haven't you seen how her eyes shine when you are in the same room?" Naman deadpanned. They both turned to me and I shrugged I had never paid any attention.

"I don't know, I never paid any attention!"

"Oh yeah, he can barely look away from Trish to see anyone else!" Naman sighed.

"I still can't believe how the mighty Viraj has fallen and how in just one look Trish tamed the Casanova!" Shlok laughed and Naman joined him.

I smiled because that was true.

I could have never imagined my life would turn around so beautifully. She was all that mattered to me, she was all I wanted in my life!

All three of us came from broken homes. My parents were sort of together, of course keep aside the occasional flings my dad kept having but they were not close to me. Shlok's parents could barely stand each other, though they continued to live together in the same house, while Naman's mom died giving birth to him and he never knew a mother's love.

All three of us despised the home situation and though we never said it out loud somewhere deep within none of us was very keen on marrying or settling down. We were happy with our carefree bachelor days, had fewer responsibilities as we built our careers, had occasional flings or one-night stands to just get the steam out, and never wanted to commit to one person like I had now.

Now, that she had changed my life and I loved the change, I really wanted these two to see what blissful calm a right girl could bring into one's life! I wished these two found someone as wonderful as Trisha to settle down with.

# CHAPTER TWENTY

# Happy Ending or Not So Much

### *Trisha*

I gazed at my reflection in the mirror. I looked so ethereal and beautiful if I could say it myself. Ana had done an amazing job of light makeup on my face, perfect bridal makeup. I wore a baby pink and red silk saree. Baby pink colour all over with a thick heavy red border and red blouse. I knew Viraj loved pink colour on me, he had openly said so. For the wedding he wanted to design a saree for me, but I put my foot down.

Deeksha Di was adamant that groom should not see bridal outfit before the wedding and I pleaded him to let me buy one on my own. Deeksha Di, Ana and I had the best time of our lives purchasing our sarees for the wedding.

Ana wanted three identical sarees but Di chastised her saying, mine would be the most exquisite and heavy one because I was the bride. So, both of them bought lighter silk sarees to wear. Di was going to reach the court with Jiju directly dressed in a dark green coloured saree she had purchased for herself, while Ana bought a dark brown saree for herself. Ana and I helped each other get dressed then she applied makeup on herself first then did mine too. Her hair was short while I had long hair, so she made a bun for me and decked it up with flowers as well.

"You look wow, Trish! Let me click a few pics!"

"Come we will take a selfie!"

"No, let me first take a few of yours fully, with your saree and everything. Bhaiya is going to be smitten all over again!"

She laughed and I hid my face as my cheeks heated up. He had been looking forward to the first night far more than the wedding itself.

Weirdo!

Shlok was coming to pick us up in his car for the court, while Viraj was to reach the court himself. Yuvi had promised to bring the garlands.

"Wow, Trish! You look lovely, welcome to our world!" Shlok kissed my head and pulled me in a side hug. "Viraj is so lucky to have you by his side and we are all blessed, now that you will take care of him, we can relax easily!"

I laughed. I was wondering as to how Shlok was talking seriously. He was the fun-loving guy of the trio always hiding behind happy banter and cheerful face. I had often seen something dark and troublesome in his eyes but he masked it well.

"How do I look?" Ana asked from behind and he turned to look at her. He stilled while she blushed profusely.

"You look lovely!" He spoke but his voice came out a husky whisper and I narrowed my eyes.

She blushed some more and walked towards the door without giving him a second glance.

What just happened here?

As we locked the house and turned to sit in Shlok's car, Ana sat in the front leaving me and Shlok looking at each other.

"Thanks for coming to pick us up!"

"My pleasure, Trish! Anytime anything you need; I am just a call away. I will come no matter whatever time of the day it is!" He said earnestly and my heart melted a little.

These two guys had adopted me fully into their folds just because Viraj loved me and was marrying me now. This is what having true friends felt like.

Ana kept asking Shlok a lot of questions and I relaxed at the backseat, trying to focus on the road and not on her chatter.

Today was going to be the biggest day of my life, I was finally going to marry Viraj and how beautifully he had changed my life. A year back, I couldn't have imagined marrying one of the most eligible bachelors of the country. Even when I had started working for him, I had been scared of him, of the reasons he was stalking me and of what he would do to me, if he found me alone somewhere.

But over the past year, all he had done was heal me, take away the broken pieces and make me whole again. He taught me design; he taught me how to stand up for myself and how to be a better person. Like the perfect partner he helped me grow! And today I was going to become Trisha Viraj Rajvansh. I had no qualms about dropping my surname or taking on his.

"Trish, share your live location with Viraj, please!" Shlok's loud voice jolted me out of my thoughts and I sat up a little straighter. Did he just ask me to share our location with Viraj?

"Why?" I blurted.

"Just do it, please!"

"Don't tell me bhaiya is getting so impatient that he needs to track Trish now." Ana asked and I laughed as I shared the live location with him.

Shlok suddenly took a sharp left turn and I swirled behind in the seat.

"Woah!" Ana screeched.

"We had to go straight!" I looked around baffled.

"I know, someone is following us!" Shlok mumbled and dialled a number, the phone connecting to his car's Bluetooth.

Ana and I sat frozen for a few seconds digesting his words and then both of us frantically looked back to see who was following us. Why would anyone follow us? And what for?

"Naman, Trish has shared our live location with Viraj, get someone to cover us, someone is on our tail."

"Shit! Drive safe!"

"Yes, you get on the job, man!"

"Which car are you in?" Viraj's voice came from behind. They were all together, why was he asking about the car model? What was going on?

"In my Kushaq, I will keep her safe!"

He disconnected the call.

"Keep her safe? What about me?" Ana alleged in a shocked tone.

"Yeah, you as well!" He groaned and his gaze met mine in the rear-view mirror. Two black SUVs were behind us.

"Why would anyone follow us?"

"There are things you don't know yet, Trish. We found out only early today morning."

"What?"

"Relax, you are safe. I promise, we will get to Viraj."

I nodded.

I trusted him, but worry began to gawk at my insides, what did he mean by things I didn't know. Was there a threat? But who would bother about me or Ana? Threat to Viraj, perhaps, he came from an affluent background. Naman and Viraj knew something because Naman had not once asked about details, and all Viraj had asked was which car, how would that matter?

I was lost in my thoughts looking ahead as Shlok drove expertly weaving us out of traffic, but we were now going in the opposite direction from Bandra.

"What's going on Trish? Shlok?" Ana hissed as confused as me.

"Please, let me focus!" He snapped back at her and she glared at him. He didn't even realize she was glaring at him as he was focused on driving at full speed and looking in the rear-view mirror for the car behind.

"Trish, you are wearing seat belt, right?" Shlok suddenly screamed and before I could reply in affirmative a car banged hard into our car and I jerked forward. Thank God for the seatbelt else,

I would have snapped my neck in two by now. Ana shrieked in shock and Shlok's hand shot out in front of her to protect her, as he accelerated further.

"Both okay?" He asked.

"Yes!"

"Yes!"

"Damn, my new car!" He mumbled eliciting a giggle from Ana and finally he glared at her.

The SUV behind us rammed into us yet again and we all jerked forward.

"I am scared, what's going on?" Ana whispered her voice shaky.

"Sit tight, princess, I am trying to save us all." Shlok replied.

"Please I don't want to die!"

"Neither do I."

Shlok picked up speed instead of slowing down even a bit. Someone was trying to hurt us all and Shlok was determined to keep his promise. Ana was shivering with fear in the front now as I felt a chill run down my spine. Would I get to see Viraj? Would I ever get to be his wife? Or was the best day of my life going to be the last?

I looked back and saw the SUV come charging towards us to ram into us yet again, but before the car could hit us a third time, I saw another car block its way horizontally, a red SUV, shucks Viraj!

The cars all came to a stop and were immediately surrounded by the Police. Amidst the police sirens, Naman opened the car door for me, while Yuvi pulled Ana out. She immediately clung to him, as she sobbed like a baby, hiding her face in his chest. I ran towards the red SUV; Viraj was still inside. His car was damaged beyond recognition. Shlok and Naman pulled open Viraj's door and he stumbled out, looking a little disoriented but unhurt.

I leapt forward and he caught me in his arms. He was fine, I was with him, finally.

"You, okay?" He cupped my face and surveyed my body for injuries.

"I am fine, Shlok kept me safe! But you?"

"I am good, see I am all good!" He pulled me in a hug as I broke down and tears rolled down my face. "Shhh, don't cry baby, we are all good, you look so beautiful, just like my angel!"

I laughed amid the tears.

Ana walked towards us, and Viraj opened his arms for her and she hugged us both together.

"I was so scared!"

"We are all fine! Thanks to Viraj and Shlok!" I patted her back.

Shlok put a hand on my head and turned around to talk to the police officer. We sat in Shlok's car for a while with Yuvi as Viraj, Shlok, and Naman spoke to the police and then they all came smiling and hugging each other.

"Let's get married, baby!" Viraj declared and everyone burst into laughter.

"What just happened?"

"I will tell you everything, but not now, if we are late, we won't be able to get married today and I do not want to wait any longer!" He declared making Ana giggle, all the boys burst into fits of laughter and I hid my face with both my palms.

Viraj's car was damaged and had to be towed away. Shlok's car had taken a bad beating but it could still be driven. We all settled in his and Naman's car and went towards the court, where an anxious Deeksha Di paced outside the registrar's hall.

"Why? How are you all coming together?" She ran to me as soon as we got out of the car.

"Small accident, nothing major, let's go inside, else we will miss our slot!" Viraj pacified her, took my hand in his, and ran towards the hall, only to realize I couldn't run with him in the saree.

He bent picked me up bridal style and entered the registrar's office to witness a bunch of curious gazes from strangers and uncontrolled laughter from members of my family trailing behind. The marriage itself was uneventful and we got Deeksha Di, Shlok, and Yuvi to sign for us, as witnesses while Naman signed as our lawyer.

We all went out to a nightclub, these guys frequented often to celebrate our wedding. Viraj had proposed a dinner, but Shlok, Yuvi and Ana wanted to go the nightclub and dance the night away. Raj Jiju also seemed interested, while Di and Naman were happy as long as we celebrated our wedding, so here we were in a loud noisy nightclub.

We all had earlier gone to Viraj's house, where we had shifted most of Ana and my stuff the day before, we all got changed. Viraj pulled me into his room and fulfilled his fantasy of peeling away my saree. He had pushed me up against a wall, as soon as the last shred of cloth dropped from my body and had taken me hard and rough, grunting that he couldn't wait even a moment longer. I didn't want him to wait. I was drenched and aching for him.

"Against the wall, first time as husband and wife, damn. I should have done better!"

"Oh, it was so good, what do you mean by better!" I sighed as he put me back on my feet and I quickly sat down on the bed, lest I fall.

"I love you, Trish!"

"I love you, Viraj, why did you put your life in danger for us?"

"I would do it all over again, but now there is no danger. It's all been taken care of!"

"Who was it? What happened?"

"Not today, Trish. Let's enjoy our special day. I promise I will tell you everything, but can you please keep the worry aside just for today, for me?"

I nodded. I could do anything for him.

"Come on Ana, you can do this!" Shlok cheered on, as she got ready to take the shots with everyone else.

Viraj, Deeksha Di and I sat and watched them, as we three had stuck with our mocktails, while Raj Jiju, Yuvi, and Shlok seemed to compete with each other as to who could get more drunk.

"He has seen my dad and still no use!" Di gruntled looking at Rajveer Jiju and I covered her hand with mine.

"Let him enjoy, tonight, Di. It's not like he drinks every day!"

"No, that he doesn't." She shuddered.

Naman stopped after two shots and pulled Ana away too.

"I want more."

"No, I can't carry around so many drunks!"

"These people can..." She slurred slightly pointing at us and Di and I groaned realizing she was drunk already.

"No, Viraj will only carry Trisha tonight. You sit here!" He pushed her toward our booth.

"I want more!"

"Okay, I will get you a drink, but no more shots." Viraj walked over to her.

"Bhaiya!" She hugged him and Naman made a face only to be chastised by Viraj.

Viraj brought her a mocktail and made her sit next to Di. A waiter brought food to our booth and Viraj made Ana eat some forcefully too.

After midnight, Viraj and Naman drove around dropping everyone home before we could get back to ours. I helped Ana change and get to bed first and then I came into our bedroom, to find, that Viraj had managed to put up some bouquets in the room and rose petals on the bed.

"Welcome in my life, angel!"

"Aww... when did you do all this?"

"I had got the bouquets delivered earlier today and kept them hidden. This I did just now!"

"Oh, Viraj, you are too good for me!"

"No, angel, you saved me. You changed my life for the best and I will spend the rest of my life cherishing you for agreeing to spend your life with me." He nuzzled his nose in my neck and I was lost in the sensations.

I sighed; how did he manage to say such nice things!

"I love you!"

"I love you more! I am so glad I decided to stalk my love..."

# Epilogue

## *Viraj*

<hr>

Last week was crazy with our wedding and all the visits to the police station and the court as well, so much so that we all needed a break now, so Trisha and I decided to come to Goa with the entire gang instead of just us sneaking away for our honeymoon.

"All our life is a honeymoon, Viraj, if we are together. But they all deserve a break as much as us."

"I agree!"

And just like that our plan was made and here we were all sprawled out in the gorgeous golden sand of South Goa, in front of a majestic Air BnB cottage that we had rented.

Shlok, Naman, Rajveer, Yuvi and I lay in the sun while the sisters sat under the shade of the tree gossiping among themselves. Their laughter often reached us making all of us sigh in relief to see them relaxed after everything that unravelled last week. Rajveer didn't know much about the car chase and the things that had led to it, and he didn't care either.

Just the night before our wedding, Naman cracked open the entire case and found the proofs he had been looking for. There was just one person behind Trisha's Activa accident and her dad's death.

Vikash Rajvansh, my uncle.

Rohit had been crushing over Trisha and waiting to get to know her but before he could approach her, he noticed that she was growing close to me and had befriended even my friends, in a fit of rage he blurted it all to Vikash Uncle when he had come to office one day. Vikash uncle saw her leaving my cabin and then going to the basement to leave on her bike. He followed her in his black Audi and rammed into her just as she was about to stop at a signal and cruised away at full speed before he could be caught. Yuvi had spotted that scratch, the one Trisha had drawn on his parked car in our house, when he was cleaning his bike one morning and called up, Naman, thus solving one of the puzzle pieces.

Vikash uncle always felt he was the second fiddle in the Rajvansh household and in the business empire, while he wanted to be equal to the man in control, my dad. But my dad was far more aggressive and uncle could never rebel against him and lived all his life in my dad's shadows. When it came to the next generation to take up the mantle, though Rohit and I were equally qualified, my dad declared me the CEO and it was I who decided to make Rohit the CFO of the company.

Vikash uncle was convinced in his mind that Rohit would also always remain in my shadows and would never be able to come out on top, and he wanted that to change. So, he started helping Rohit on the side to be better and to outsmart me, without leaving any clues for me or Dad to pick up. Rohit always sidled with my dad, ensuring that he was in my dad's good books.

I gave them the perfect opportunity to oust me on a golden platter when I kissed Trisha in Shlok's party. Rohit went and rattled to my dad and spun the story in such a way that Dad impulsively kicked Trisha out of the company. It was the vile words injected in my father's mind by my uncle and Rohit that dad went on to humiliate her as well, which led to our showdown and me leaving the house and the company.

That should have been the end of it all, after all, Rohit had got full control of the Rajvansh group, but when I launched my own brand, Dad started following my career again and tracking my progress closely. So, they took my dad to show the neighbourhood where Trisha lived, to make him realize that I was a lost cause and this girl was out to end her poverty.

The CCTV footage showed Dad and Rohit, while they were checking out Trisha's home and her lane, Uncle noticed her dad walking towards the house. He stopped him midway, made small talk, and gave him 10000 rupees in cash, which he had been carrying for some other transaction, making her father turn back to the liquor shop, and my dad never even saw her father. Probably, my uncle had not anticipated that her father would die of overdosing on alcohol, but one doesn't know what he was thinking. He accepted that he only wanted to show my dad that Trisha's father asked for money when he understood Vikash uncle was related to me.

My dad had been very restless since the time I declared I was marrying Trisha; he didn't want it but he couldn't do much to stop it either because I had his videotapes. He mentioned to Uncle that he wasn't happy about me marrying Trisha, without obviously uttering anything about the tapes and Uncle hatched yet another plan. He decided to hit where it would hurt me the most and thereby cause further damage to the father-son relationship.

For my uncle, whom I married didn't matter, but it mattered to my dad and the first person I would blame after Trisha's accident or death would be my father making any reconciliation between us impossible.

Naman and I had suspected Rohit all along, and not once did I think my uncle, who had brought me up, just like Rohit, would go to all this extent just to get Rohit to have it all and to alienate me from the family.

Rohit had been devastated when his father was arrested. My dad had even come to plead with me to take the complaints back and to not press criminal charges but I was done with all this petty politics. Criminal charges were pressed, though we asked for leniency given his age and his health conditions.

Rohit had asked me if I wanted to take back the CEO role, and I had declined. I never had any intentions of returning and they went to all this length for a waste. I was always secure and happy in creating my own world. My dad finally released my personal bank account and let me have access to it last week, realizing that he was also to blame for having acted in haste and under the influence of my uncle.

I sat lost in my thoughts when I heard laughter ring out. Trisha and Deeksha were walking towards us. Deeksha led the way with a tray full of beer and soft drink cans, while Trisha with a tray of snacks trailed behind her. I sat up straight at their sight and Rajveer moved his legs to I think make way for them, but Deeksha tripped on his feet and fell forward. I jerked forward but was too far to do anything and she crashed on top of a sleeping Naman, with the cans flying across some landing on Shlok, and one landing straight on Yuvi's face. All of them were fast asleep and shrieked at the sudden attack. I laughed at their plight.

Naman opened his eyes and the first thing he saw was a head full of hair on his bare chest and he grumbled.

"Ana!"

Rajveer rushed forward to help Deeksha get up and Naman looked at her horrified. He had not realized it was the married sister who had fallen on him, while her husband looked on and had just assumed it was Ana. Ana kept tripping and falling, even dropping things all the time.

"I am sorry, what happened?" He asked when he realized who was on top of him.

By now Shlok and Yuvi also sat straight looking at the mess. Deeksha was so flustered that she wouldn't meet anyone's eye and, in her haste, to get away from Naman she slipped as she got up and fell back on him making him groan yet again.

"What the fuck, Dee, can't you see?" Rajveer yelled and she shuddered. Naman and I looked at each other. Naman held her hand while Shlok helped her stand up straight. She turned mumbled an apology and rushed inside the house.

"Why did you yell at her, man, she fell because you moved suddenly!" I spat out at Rajveer.

"I was just making way!"

"Yeah, but she tripped over your leg because you moved at the last minute, she didn't decide to go jump on Naman on her own!"

"Yeah, whatever!" He mumbled and went inside the cottage.

"She fell on him but why was I attacked with these cans?" Shlok grumbled rubbing his bare chest. Trisha laughed behind me, reminding me, that she stood still since the entire circus began unfolding here.

Yuvi and Ana collected all the cans, while I took the snack tray from her and we all settled down on the sand chatting. Trisha leaned into me and I put a hand around her shoulder. We were chatting, when Deeksha came out of the cottage with her eyes swollen red. Had she been crying?

"Are you okay?" I asked and she nodded, sitting next to Trisha.

"Where is he?" Naman asked, his gaze alarmed he had noticed the red eyes too.

"He is taking a nap inside!" She spoke still not looking at Naman or anyone else.

"I feel like eating Masala Papad!" Shlok grumbled, trying to change the topic.

"Yeah, there is a pack of Papad kept in the pantry!" Deeksha finally declared looking up at Shlok.

"I will make it and bring it!" Ana stood up and we all looked at her horrified. She just couldn't cook anything; Trisha had told me several times.

"Do you even know how to make it?" Shlok asked her sarcastically and her face fell.

"You sit, or you'll burn down the cottage!" Yuvi laughed.

Ana made a face at Yuvi and walked inside. Trisha got up to go behind her.

"Wait, let her!" I pulled her back down.

"What has come over her today?" Yuvi wondered.

"Because Shlok asked!" Naman mumbled and I kicked him hard.

"What did you say, Naman?" Trisha asked.

"Nothing, I was just saying, let her make!" Naman replied and Shlok rolled his eyes.

We kept chatting among ourselves, Yuvi narrating his college escapades and adventures with his professors when a loud blast shook us all.

"Shit!" Shlok was facing towards it and stood up, all colour drained off his face.

I turned to see our BnB cottage on fire.

"Ana!" Trisha rushed forward.

"Raj!" Deeksha shrieked and ran.

"Wait!" Naman yelled and ran forward. Shlok and Yuvi both sprinted ahead while I caught both the sisters in a tight hug, telling them to let the guys get Ana and Rajveer out.

"You both stay here; they will get them out!" I spoke as I saw Yuvi, Shlok and Naman enter the cottage.

"Raj is inside, he is sleeping!" Deeksha pushed hard at my chest and ran forward.

"Di!" Trisha yelled after her and before I could run forward to stop her, Trisha's weight fell on me. I looked down to realize she had fainted.

"Trish!" I shook her but she was dead to the world.

I saw my whole world come crashing down in front of me as the fire raged on and there was no sight of anyone coming out.

--- The End ---